As Cl
she was

It was so pote...
breath away.

"Something wrong?" he asked. "You're flushed."

Her hands went to her cheeks. "Must be the heat from the stove."

She'd lied. It wasn't that. It was heat…but from Brady himself.

Because when she got close to him she felt her body tighten, her pulse speed up and a low coil of reaction in her belly.

All signs that were familiar.

All signs she remembered.

How could this be? She didn't understand. Why was she *aroused* by Brady's nearness, the male smell of him, the physical presence of him!

Brady, her best friend?

Dear Reader,

A Man She Couldn't Forget is a combination of plotlines
I've enjoyed as a reader. First, the story deals with amnesia.
I researched the malady and it fit nicely into this plot.
Next, there is a friends-to-lovers angle. It's fun to develop
characters who know each other, then fall in love—and are
shocked by it! Finally, I like the concept of a love triangle,
although I hadn't realized how tricky it would be.

Another challenge was the characterization. The hero,
Brady Langston, jumped off the pages—sexy, artistic,
fun loving and head over heels about Clare. However,
I did struggle with finding a way for the reader to know
Clare when she doesn't know herself. I hate dumping
information in, so instead I filtered her personality into
conversations, while giving a bit of background.

Last, Jonathan, the "other man," had to be likable, though
not *too* likable. What kind of heroine would Clare be if she
was involved with someone who didn't appeal to readers?

Of course, Brady and Clare are meant to be and the best
part is that she somehow knows it even when she can't
remember him. Hopefully, her dawning awareness will keep
you reading.

The story also has books. Brady writes children's stories,
while Clare writes cookbooks. By the way, my own family
has passed the recipes in this book through generations,
or they have created them after great trial and error.
(It took my sister twenty-one tries to get the minestrone
right.) You can find these recipes on my Web site at
www.kathrynshay.com. Visit my blog there, and e-mail
me through the site or at kshayweb@rochester.rr.com.

I hope you love Brady and Clare and their very
complicated but heartwarming story.

Kathy Shay

A MAN SHE COULDN'T FORGET

Kathryn Shay

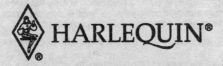

HARLEQUIN®

TORONTO • NEW YORK • LONDON
AMSTERDAM • PARIS • SYDNEY • HAMBURG
STOCKHOLM • ATHENS • TOKYO • MILAN • MADRID
PRAGUE • WARSAW • BUDAPEST • AUCKLAND

Recycling programs
for this product may
not exist in your area.

ISBN-13: 978-0-373-71538-1
ISBN-10:   0-373-71538-2

A MAN SHE COULDN'T FORGET

www.eHarlequin.com

Printed in U.S.A.

ABOUT THE AUTHOR

Kathryn Shay is the author of twenty-three Harlequin Superromance books and nine novels and two novellas from the Berkley Publishing Group. She has won several awards. Among them are five *Romantic Times BOOKreviews* awards, three Holt Medallions, three Desert Quill awards and a Booksellers' Best Award. A former high school teacher, she lives in upstate New York, where she sets many of her stories.

Books by Kathryn Shay

HARLEQUIN SUPERROMANCE

To my sister Joanie.
Thanks for the recipes in this book, for watching
numerous cooking shows with me and for enduring
all those amnesia movies!
I love you.

CHAPTER ONE

AS THE CAR PULLED INTO the driveway of a huge Victorian house with peaked roofs, slate-blue siding and luscious landscaping, Clare Boneli stared at the sprawling structure without a shred of recognition. A quick burst of panic shot through her, and her breathing sped up. The darkness inside her yawned, widened, threatened to take her under.

"It's all right, Clarissa. Everything's going to be fine."

The man beside her spoke the soothing words, her panic abated somewhat. It went away more quickly now than it had before. When Clare had first awakened from the coma a week ago, she hadn't even known her name. That had come back suddenly, unlike the memories of her past.

She managed to choke out, "This is where I live?"

"Yes." Jonathan, who'd been at her bedside most days over the past two weeks, smiled sadly. He was dressed in an impeccable gray suit and pristine white shirt. He'd told her he owned the TV station they said she worked for.

And more. They were dating. Seriously, for over a year. But try as she might, Clare couldn't remember him or this beautiful house or anything else about her life. Panic threatened again, and she grabbed for his hand.

"I don't remember," she murmured.

He linked their fingers. Even his touch was foreign.

How could she not recognize someone she'd been so close to? Someone, he'd told her, she'd been intimate with? Shouldn't she sense things about him? Again, her heart began to pound, like it always did when she tried to make herself remember and couldn't.

"You're going to be fine. It'll all come back. Dr. Montgomery thinks when you're in your own environment, familiar things will jog your memory."

Retrograde amnesia, the neurologist had told her. *The loss of memory of events that occur before a trauma. Usually it lasts a few hours.*

In Clare's case, the trauma had been a car accident on a rainy morning at two a.m. She'd crashed into a guardrail, lurched forward and banged her face on the steering wheel. Her head had ricocheted to the side, resulting in a huge bump on her skull and injuring her brain. Once the swelling had gone down, the tests revealed no permanent brain damage, and the doctors expected her memory to return soon. But it hadn't. So she'd been referred to a psychiatrist, Anna Summers, whom she'd seen twice and would continue to see now that she had been released.

"Dr. Summers told me that sometimes it takes a while for memories to come back, even if there's no visible brain damage."

"As I said, I think being home will help." He scowled. "I wish I didn't have to go out of town today. It's just that I postponed meetings in Chicago three times when you were in the hospital."

"Of course you have to go. You put everything on hold for me."

"I wanted to."

She peered out the window again. The late-afternoon

June sun sparkled off the black shingles on the roof and the many windows of the exterior. "Tell me about my condo before we go inside."

"Your favorite room is the kitchen."

Still facing away from him, she sighed. "Because I'm a chef, right?"

"The best."

They'd told her a few things in the hospital so she wouldn't go into shock when she got back to her life. She lived in Rockford, a medium-sized town in upstate New York, and was a chef and successful cookbook author. Jonathan was WRNY's station owner and had offered her a cooking show, *Clarissa's Kitchen,* three years ago. Her parents were dead, she had a sister who lived in Arizona— a teacher, divorced, no children. And though Clare was thirty-six, she wasn't married. She wondered why.

Jonathan kept hold of her hand. "Let's go inside."

"In a minute." Stalling, she pulled down the visor and opened the mirror to check her appearance, briefly wondering if she was vain. What stared back at her was a stranger with green eyes and short sandy-blond hair. Again the lack of recognition shocked her, and she had to take in deep breaths.

"Can you tell your hair's different?" he asked.

She shook her head. "No." But she knew it had been long. In the hospital, the doctors had to cut away a chunk of it on the left side and shave the area to take care of the bump on her head. When she awoke from the coma, Jonathan brought in the town's best stylist to cut it flatteringly. "Did I like my hair long?"

"Yes. I think the short style suits you better, though. It's more sophisticated."

Closing the visor, she smoothed down the peach sundress she wore. It was beautiful and expensive, she could tell. Someone had brought it to the hospital, but she didn't know who.

Jonathan smiled at her encouragingly. "Ready now?"

"I guess."

They got out of his car, which she recognized was a Jag. It was funny how she knew things like that. She had what the doctors called episodic amnesia, where she didn't remember past events but could remember objects and procedural things, like how to change a lightbulb or take a bus.

As they walked up the brick path to the front porch, they passed a profusion of big fat peonies, petunias and geraniums. Pots of the latter variety hung from the rafters, she noticed as they climbed the steps. Warmth seeped into her at the sight of them and as she reached the house; the remnants of fear abated. She felt comfortable here.

The double wooden front doors had a digital lock, and Jonathan keyed in some numbers.

"You know the combination?" she asked.

"Yes." So they must be close, as he said. "I come here often."

When they stepped inside, she took in the huge foyer with an exquisite Persian rug on the hardwood floors, a breathtaking solid oak staircase and large windows. Again, calm infused her.

"Clarissa," Jonathan said gently. "Are you all right? Is this too much?"

"No, not at all. Just give me a minute." She looked around at the first floor. "There are four condos in the house, right?"

"Yes. Two on the first and two on the second. There's

also an attic of sorts." He added the last with a note of displeasure tingeing his voice.

"I live on the second floor."

Jonathan smiled. It was a nice smile, though forced sometimes; often it didn't reach his hazel eyes. She guessed her not remembering him had been hard to take. "You knew that."

"Nothing else, though."

He kissed her forehead. "That's enough for now. Just be glad familiar things are already jogging your memory."

Taking her hand again, he led her over to the elevator. She caught another glimpse of the staircase that spiraled upward and had a quick vision of dark hair and startling blue eyes. "Brady, the other man who came to the hospital every day? He lives here, right?"

Jonathan's face hardened. "Yes."

Suddenly, she saw herself, carrying grocery bags, climbing those steps.

And the memory of someone teasing her. *Elevators are for older people and the ill. I never take it, but if that's the kind of girl you are...*

The voice belonged to Brady.

The elevator pinged, and she and Jonathan entered the car. They rode in silence, and when it stopped, they exited on the second floor. The first thing she noticed was color on the walls. A variety of sketches lined the hallway. As she got closer she saw they were illustrations done mostly in colored pencil: a couple of cartoons that made her laugh, an adorable mouse and rat in some kind of square off, a picture of a dish of piping hot lasagna, a green salad and a wine bottle. Dull pain began to form in her head. She raised her hands to her temples. "Oh."

"What's wrong?"

"Some pain for a second. It's gone now."

Jonathan stared at the sketches. Glared, really. "Too much too soon."

He grasped her arm and led her down a corridor to condo number three. Number four was next to hers, their doors side by side. Hers sported a simple wreath of silk flowers, but the other one had been painted like a mural. The light-blue background was broken by white puffy clouds; birds fluttered over the door, all done in the same style as the illustrations on the wall. She imagined that when the door opened, the birds would seem to be flying. On closer examination, the little feathery creatures had...personalities. One blue jay sported a baseball cap and winked. A goldfinch had an apron tied around its body and held a spatula. There was a sparrow with a baby bird, and a robin in a suit.

Tension coiled inside her. "Who did this? And the sketches on the walls?"

Before Jonathan could answer, the door to number three—her place—swung open. Inside her condo stood Brady Langston. His grin was big and broad and genuine. Though he wasn't any taller than Jonathan, his muscular stature made it seem as though he towered over them both. When he'd been at her bedside in the hospital, she'd found his presence soothing. When he held her hand, that, too, felt right. "There you are. I thought I heard voices."

"What the hell are you doing here?" Jonathan asked.

Brady's brows raised. "I'm the welcome wagon, Harris."

A quick glance told her Jonathan's light complexion was flushed. "I have home health-care aides scheduled to be with Clarissa around the clock while I'm gone."

Brady squared his shoulders—they were big and broad, too. Jonathan mirrored the gesture. Clare didn't need her memory to feel the animosity crackle between them. And it made her stomach clench.

"I sent the woman who showed up home," Brady said. "Aides are for people who don't have family and friends. We've all arranged to be here at various times, so Clare doesn't have to surround herself with strangers. And her sister is coming in when she gets back from France."

Which was why, apparently, Clare's only blood relative hadn't come to her bedside. Despite the explanation that Cathy was in Europe, Clare had wondered about that.

Fists curled at his sides, Jonathan asked, "What gave you the right to decide all this, Langston?"

Brady's palm hit the doorjamb hard.

At the sound of the slap, blinding pain shot through Clare's skull. Leaning into the wall, she closed her eyes. Brady reached out and touched her arm. "Clare, baby, you okay?"

"Now look what you've done." She heard Jonathan's voice but it was far away. "Come on, Clarissa, let's get you to bed."

Eyes still shut, her stomach roiling, she could only brace herself against the wall. Then she felt strong arms slide beneath her legs and around her back. She was picked up and cuddled to a warm, hard body. Nosing into his shirt, burying her head in his chest, she breathed in his scent. It was familiar and calmed her dramatically.

She felt herself being carried and heard mumbling behind her, but she closed it off and reveled in the safety of being in this man's arms. It was something she hadn't truly felt since she'd woken up in that hospital and recognized nothing.

Soon, she was set on a bed and covered. "Sleep, sweetheart," Jonathan mumbled.

No, wait, that wasn't Jonathan's voice. She pried her eyes open. Brady stood over her bed. And in her gut, she realized she knew this man well. Very well. But her lids got heavy and closed on their own. Maybe she could figure all this out when she awoke. Lips brushed her forehead just before she drifted off.

FOR CLARE'S SAKE, BRADY TRIED to collect himself before he left her bedroom. At least Harris had waited out in the living room and not upset her anymore with this aide thing. Taking deep breaths, Brady knew the guy would go on the attack with him—Brady would do the same if their roles were reversed—so he prepared for a fight but preferred to be in control.

He found Harris staring out the big bay window in the back, on his phone, of course. "Yes, I'll be there late afternoon. Tell the Chef's Delight people my plane leaves in ninety minutes."

When the guy clicked off, Brady spoke. "You can go anytime, Harris. I got it here."

Harris spun around, and there was fire in his eyes. So Brady tried even harder to stay cool. Rocking back on his heels, he stuck his hands in his jeans pockets.

"What the hell are you trying to pull, Langston?"

Innocently, he raised his eyebrows. "Nothing. I'm Clare's best friend. I've made arrangements to take care of her."

"You may have been her best friend before, but we both know things changed over the last year." Harris started to punch in a number on the phone. "I'm getting the aides back."

"Not after you see this." Feeling smug, Brady turned away and strode into Clare's office off the living room. He found what he was looking for in the tray of her fax machine. He'd gotten the form in case Harris tried to pull something. Brady skimmed it to be certain Clare's sister, Catherine, had done what he'd asked. She'd been thousands of miles away when the accident had occurred, shocked and frustrated when he'd called…

"OH MY GOD, IS SHE OKAY?"

"She doesn't remember anything."

"Brady, I can't come home from France. I'm with fifteen people who depend on me."

"You don't have to come home. I'll take care of her. But I need something from you."

After he told her what, she asked, "Why do you want to do this, Brady?"

"Because we're her friends."

"I know, but after what she did to all of you. To all of us."

"None of that matters. And she needs you now, too."

"I know. I wish I could come back sooner."

"Leave it to me, Cath. Send the fax, and come to Rockford when you get back…"

QUICKLY, HE READ THE SHEET of paper. Perfect. He left the den, crossed to Harris and handed it to him.

"What's this?"

"A notarized directive from Clare's sister, who's her only living relative and has power of attorney in case something happens to Clare."

Harris cocked his head. "I thought they were estranged. That's why I've never met her."

"You thought wrong." Brady folded his arms over the chest of the shirt Clare had given him for Christmas one year. She thought the color matched his eyes. *He* thought it might bring him good luck. "Wrong about a lot of things, I might add."

Raising his chin, Harris scowled. "I'll have my attorneys look into this."

"You do that, Jon." A name he knew the guy hated to be called. "Meanwhile, *we'll* take care of Clare."

"Don't you dare try to keep her from seeing me when I get back from my trip."

"Go ahead, see her. We're starting with a clean slate, at least for a little while, and this time, I'm not giving up on her."

As he'd done before, which had been a huge mistake. One he'd tried to rectify the night of the accident and felt slicing guilt over now. He pushed the thought away.

Harris drew himself up to his six-foot height. If Brady were to sketch him, he'd put a sheen over him that conveyed the word *polished*. Right from his expensively styled blond hair down to his Armani suit to the wing tips on his feet. For a second, Brady glanced at his jeans and sandals. No, he wasn't going to do this again. "Shall I show you out?"

The guy spat an expletive, which only made Brady laugh at his loss of composure. But when Harris finally left, Brady stopped laughing and sank onto the expensive leather couch Clare had bought a couple of years ago. He preferred the tapestry one and matching love seat he and Max had carried up the stairs years ago.

Watch out, you're going to hurt your back.

I'm tough, babe. No worries.

She'd laughed, and cooked them all dinner that night.

God, he missed how she looked, how she smelled, how

close they'd been. He'd give anything to have those days together back.

And now he had a chance to make that happen.

JONATHAN SLID INSIDE HIS JAG but didn't start the engine, despite the plane he had to catch to meet with the people from Chef's Delight. They'd approached the station about Clarissa using their products on her show and he intended to close the deal, once more getting her exactly what she wanted. His fingers curled tightly on the steering wheel in an effort to bring himself under control. He was furious at Langston for his shenanigans. Clarissa would want a nurse, someone impersonal to take care of her needs. She wasn't the touchy-feely type they all thought she was. Delia Kramer, Max Mason and her sister, Catherine, didn't know the real Clarissa. At least the person she'd evolved into over the past few years, when she'd finally come into her own. The person she was when she was with him. No longer was she a simple chef in an ordinary restaurant or even a mildly successful writer of cookbooks. She was a star; her show on TV was considered Rockford's Rachael Ray clone. And Jonathan had big plans for Clarissa to go to the top of her profession. He'd already made inquiries about syndication. Even the brass from the Cooking Channel, the crème de la crème of food networks, had indicated some interest.

They had big plans, too, as a couple. Or he thought they had. A sick feeling in his gut at the idea of losing his chance with her immobilized him. Damn it, he'd always gotten whatever he wanted in life, and he'd gone after Clarissa with the same verve with which he'd pursued a business degree at Wharton and ownership of WRNY TV. Sure, he'd been born into a wealthy family, but he'd worked hard to get the degree. And though trust funds from his beloved grandparents had helped him buy the station, he'd put in long hours to make it successful. When Clarissa had come to work there, he'd fallen hopelessly in love with her. She was a diamond in the rough, and he'd helped her polish her exterior until she shone like a brand-new gem. She'd appreciated him for it.

He glanced at the house. Damn those people. He'd been on the verge of getting her to move out of the condo into a lovely home in a more upscale neighborhood of Rockford. Though she'd been on the fence about it, he'd bought the property and had pretty much talked her into moving there with him. That he might not get to do that with her now because of some quirky twist of fate made him sad and angry.

Forcefully, he pushed out of his mind the images of the night Clarissa had been on the expressway and her car had skidded on the slick pavement and hit a guardrail. *An unfortunate accident,* the police and papers had called it. He could barely stand the thought of her being hurt, the fact that she could have been killed.

And his part in it.

Jonathan straightened and started the engine. He wouldn't allow himself to feel responsible for what had happened to her. When guilt, deep and piercing, hit him, he forced it back as he'd done since the horrid event occurred. Instead, he'd concentrate on getting Clarissa back to her old life—the part where she remembered him, loved him. The longer her memory was kept at bay, the easier it would be for him to prove once again how good they were together.

And then he'd get Brady Langston out of the picture permanently.

CLARE WAS SMALL, AND CATHY was even smaller, both so little they could barely reach the counter in Grandma's house. Her kitchen always smelled so good, and Clare loved being there. Her favorite was the spicy sauce Grandma had on the stove, but her sister liked the cookies best.

"Come, *bambine,* you are not too young for this."

Eagerly, Clare climbed up on one stool and Cathy on the other. Mommy put them both in pretty blue dresses and Mary Janes, and Grandma had tied the tiny aprons she'd made for them over their outfits.

Cathy smiled at Grandma. Clare was three years older, so she helped take care of her sister. Outside, through the big window in the kitchen, she could see her parents, sitting on the swing, holding hands. She liked it when Mommy and Daddy brought them to Italy for a visit, especially a long one where she and Cathy would stay for a month when their parents went back to Rockford.

Grandma smoothed Clare's hair down. "This is ricotta. It's the best kind of cheese." She held out a fork, and Clare tasted it first, then Cathy.

"Hmm," Clare said, but Cathy wrinkled her nose.

"It is one of the main ingredients of lasagna."

Cathy nodded at the noodles. "They're slimy, Grandma. Do I have to touch them?"

"*Si, bambina.* A good cook uses her hands."

"I'm going to be a cook," Clare said proudly. "Just like you, Grandma."

"I'm going to be a ballerina." Cathy scrambled off the stool and did a pirouette. "I'll practice."

Grandma Boneli watched her for a minute and smiled down at Clare. "Someday, *amore mio,* you're going to be famous."

"I know." Clare reached for the noodles.

Suddenly, they started to move. Oh, God, they were forming into something, coming...alive. Snakes, they were snakes! Each poked a head up. Each had a face. One was blue-eyed. It reminded Clare of Brady. The other resembled Jonathan.

Brady-the-snake curled around her wrist tightly. At the motion, the other, Jonathan, reared up on its body and stung Clare on the cheek.

She cried out. *Help me. I don't know what to do. Please, help me.*

CHAPTER TWO

MORNING FILTERED IN THROUGH the open window—cool air, the sound of birds chirping and the smell of newly mowed grass. Pulling the covers up to her neck, Clare burrowed into the pillow and sank deeper into the mattress.

Rested, she let her mind wake up with her body. When it did, gradually, the all-too-familiar anxiety began to wash over her, like a cold stream replacing all warmth. Where was she? Her eyes snapped open.

Sage-green walls. White trim. Overhead, a fan whirred. She groped the covers—a light quilt swirled with greens and whites interspersed with tiny red lines. Amidst the burst of color, blackness threatened to drown her.

Take deep breaths, Clare. That's the best way to calm down. Someone's voice from the hospital. She didn't know whose.

So she breathed in and out, once, twice…she was settled when she reached six.

All right, all right, the facts were that she didn't remember this room, this house, these people. But her short-term memory was intact: yesterday, late afternoon, Jonathan had brought her here. They'd come upstairs and there had been a confrontation between him and Brady. Clare had gotten a blinding headache, and Brady had carried her into the bedroom; she'd fallen asleep and not awakened until now, at 8:00 a.m. The long rest wasn't unusual, as she'd slept most of the time she was in the hospital. Suddenly, she remembered the dream she'd had. She was cooking with an older woman, and her sister was there. Then there was something else. Something about snakes. She shivered, and her stomach knotted. She didn't want to remember the dream, hadn't wanted to remember the ones she'd had in the hospital, either. Her therapist had explained why…

Dreams are indicative of what you're not remembering. To keep you happy, or sometimes sane, your conscious mind won't let you recall incidents in your past. In cases of amnesia, the drive is even stronger. Psychologically you're hiding what you don't want to, or can't, remember.

Was that true for her? Clare wondered. Was the cause of her amnesia psychological? It didn't have to be. The workings of the brain were still somewhat of a mystery to doctors and researchers alike, especially when amnesia was involved. Her physicians had told Clare that the cause of her memory loss could very well be physical, even if her CT scans showed no residual brain damage from the bump on her head. Damn, not even knowing why she couldn't remember things was frustrating.

Turning over, she pushed herself to a seated position and took in the rest of the room. Gleaming hardwood floors. A bank of windows overlooking the side and back yards. An adjoining room—the bathroom, probably.

Was she alone? Probably not. Brady said he and his friends—her friends, too—were going to take turns staying with her. She wished he had been here when she'd first woken up. Yesterday, just being near him had calmed her fears and anxieties. He must be a big part of the history she couldn't remember.

Then she shook her head. Now that she had regained some of her physical strength, she should stop depending on anybody too much. She sensed that wasn't her style. But fear and distress came too suddenly, too unexpectedly, and made her weak. Oh, well, no sense whining about it. Throwing back the cover, she slid out of bed and noticed she still wore her dress. The fabric was wrinkled, and she felt grungy, so she made her way to the bathroom.

It was huge. Windows lining the walls about a foot over her head, long and uncovered, let in the light but gave complete privacy. There was a dressing area to the right. A shower stall was on the left, made of light-blue fiberglass with a frosted glass door.

She stripped, turned on the faucet and stepped under the spray. It was heavenly, and for a few seconds she remembered being in this enclosed space; then the memory was gone. Squeezing shampoo from a bottle in the shower caddy, she washed her hair and luxuriated in the process and the scent of lavender surrounding her—that, too, was familiar. Gingerly, she touched the injured area. Sometimes it still ached.

Done in the shower, she crossed to the dressing room, admiring the vanity, the wooden chest of drawers and the closet.

From the latter, she chose pink capris and a white T-shirt. When she opened the underwear drawer—it was the first one she tried—she stopped short. Well, she liked pretty things. Sexy ones. Picking up a pair of leopard bikinis, she had a startling flash of a man taking the panties and a matching bra off her. It was a pleasant image and filled her with warmth, but it was gone too quickly. Whose hands were they? Jonathan's? Or those of another man she was involved with before she met him? Would she ever remember being intimate with someone? How could she forget *that?* Dr. Summers had cautioned her that in some amnesiac cases, memory didn't return. The notion chilled her and she dressed quickly.

The mirror reflected a stranger again, and fear started to coil inside her, but she forced herself to stay detached and examine her face. The bruises under her eyes were better today. Automatically she reached for a box, knowing cosmetics were in there. She used concealer to erase the last trace of black and was satisfied with the results.

"What the hell?" she said, and picked up the lipstick. It was pretty, and she liked it.

Then she blow-dried her hair just enough to get the water out and keep the mass of pretty waves.

Back in the bedroom, she stared at the doorway. Forcing herself to move to it, she stepped out into the hallway. It was short, and opened onto a large living room. She hadn't seen the condo last night because she'd buried her nose in Brady's chest as he carried her into the bedroom. Just the recollection of it made her feel better, and she wondered why.

The living area was one big space, demarcated by couches sectioning off a dining room that graced one end. Ceiling fans lifted the air around her, making her shiver. She snagged a sweater off a chair, where she must have left it before the accident, and slipped it on. Ahh. She recognized the scent. Her scent.

Slowly, she crossed to the doorway of another room off this one. It was her office, and sported a pink-and-blue striped couch that pulled out to a bed, she somehow knew. Her desk, bookshelves…evidence of her work. When her pulse quickened, she left without going inside. For that reason, she bypassed the kitchen, too.

There was no sign of Brady, no sign of anyone. Hmm. She walked to the windows in the back. A woman was in the yard weeding the huge garden.

Oh, Brady, thank you for digging this. I can grow all my herbs fresh for my recipes. She'd thrown her arms around him and hugged him tightly.

Hey, I helped. Another man, a very big, very handsome black man, teased her. *Don't I get a hug?*

Wow! That was a very specific memory, and it cheered her.

Since no one was obviously in the condo, maybe the woman in the garden was the one keeping Clare company this morning. Grabbing her keys and sticking them in her pocket, she headed out of the condo and down the stairs to the backyard. The morning air was cool and a bit damp. She made her way across the grass and called out when she was a few feet away, "Hello."

The woman's head jerked up, and she looked over her shoulder. Once again Clare's heart started to beat fast. Something was familiar about her, but it was the look on her face that upset Clare. Her dark brows knitted, and her mouth formed a definite frown. She wasn't happy to see Clare.

Slowly, she stood. "Hi, Clare. I'm sorry, I didn't know you were awake. Brady had an eight o'clock appointment, so I came up to stay with you. I checked on you, but you were still sleeping. I thought I'd pull a few weeds, since no one's had time to do it."

"Thanks for thinking of that."

The woman cocked her head as Clare came closer. Wide, almond-shaped eyes the color of chestnuts stared at her; hair to match swung in a short ponytail. She was dressed in pretty yellow shorts and a matching top. Clare gave her a tentative smile.

"You don't remember who I am."

"No, I'm sorry. But don't take offense. I don't remember anyone." She swallowed hard and felt emotion clog her throat.

"Not even Brady?"

"Should I?"

"Oh, dear, I don't think I'm supposed to tell you things."

Clare shrugged. "That's not exactly true. The doctor said to make sure I don't get too much information at once. But familiar people and objects are *supposed* to jog my memory. It's already happened some."

After a hesitation, the woman nodded. "I'm Delia Kramer, from the first floor."

"We're neighbors."

"Uh-huh."

"And friends?"

"Ah…yes."

"Could a friend fix me some coffee?" She glanced back at the house. "I didn't go in the kitchen yet. I'm afraid to."

Delia came out of the garden. "I'm sorry, Clare. That must be hard for you."

A flash of recognition of this woman listening to her and comforting her. "Did you always know what I was thinking? How I was feeling?"

"At one point in our lives."

Confused by the comment, Clare was about to ask for

an explanation, but Delia started walking toward the house and Clare fell into step alongside her. "I came to the hospital when you were in a coma. But the doctors didn't want too many visitors after you awakened." Another pause. "I sent flowers, carnations. Your favorites."

Clare smiled. "That's why I liked them so much."

In truth, Clare had wondered why no one had visited but Brady and Jonathan. There were flowers from others, none of whom she remembered, and a few calls after she woke up. Her sister had phoned a couple of times from France. She'd cried when Clare didn't remember her, and often had tears in her voice when she called back. Damn it, how could you not remember your own flesh and blood?

When they arrived at Delia's first floor condo, they went in through a set of French doors leading into a kitchen, which was roomy with warm wood everywhere. Because it seemed right, Clare took a stool at the island instead of the breakfast nook. Delia assembled the coffee and when it began to drip, turned around. This time, her expression was pained.

"What's wrong, Delia?"

"It's just that I haven't seen you at my kitchen island in a long time."

"No? You said we were friends. And we live in the same building."

"I—let's talk about something else. Your hair looks great short."

"Please, just tell me that one thing. Why haven't I been here in a while?"

Delia leaned against the counter and crossed her arms over her chest. "You got really busy with your cookbooks and TV show."

"But we were close before that?"

"Yes, we were college roommates, then you went to culinary school, and I got my master's degree. I'm an elementary school teacher, now."

"My sister's a teacher, too."

"I know. Cathy and I have a lot in common. Anyway, you were maid of honor in my wedding. After you finished your training, you moved here when a condo opened up because we owned one." She glanced over at a picture by the window. "You don't remember anything? Anyone?" Her voice caught on the last word.

"I have flashes. I knew I used to sit at the island." She frowned. "So I must have been here a lot." When Delia just stared at her, Clare nodded to the photo. "Is that your husband?"

"Excuse me for a minute." Her voice quivered and Delia disappeared into what looked like a powder room off the kitchen.

Standing, Clare crossed to the window and picked up the picture. It was of a man in army fatigues. Closely cropped hair. Dark eyes sparkling with mischief. He looked so young and handsome and hopeful. Oh my God, he was dead. She knew what had happened.

Delia had been at the computer when Clare had come in through the front door and into this kitchen. She remembered how bereft she'd felt but knew she had to be strong for her friend...

"HEY," DELIA SAID. "I'm e-mailing Don, but I don't know how to begin." Her hand went to her stomach. "How do you tell somebody thousands of miles away he's going to be a daddy? He'll be happy, though." She frowned. "Damn that army reserve. I told him he never should have signed on. He'd be here…"

Finally she looked up. Her face sobered. "Clare, what…" She stood and hurried over to her friend. "What is it, what's happened?"

"Dee, I'm sorry. I'm so sorry. The army people, I saw them outside approaching the front door. I told them I was your friend. I insisted they tell me first…so you wouldn't be alone…"

A knock on the door, as loud as a gunshot.

"What is it?" Delia's fingers bit into Clare's arm. "What is it?"

"Honey, I'm sorry. Don's dead…"

CLARE RECALLED WHAT she wished she hadn't…crying through the whole official announcement, days of grim reality, nights of holding her friend while she sobbed out her pain. But Delia had gotten through it, with the help of Brady, Clare and someone else. The guy helping Brady carry the couch, the guy from the garden.

Now, however, Clare felt the loss all over again. It was as if someone she knew and loved had just died, making Clare take in a quick breath.

She heard Delia move behind her. "What are you doing?"

Setting down the frame, Clare turned around. "I remember. I'm so sorry."

"You look so sad. Do you remember Don himself?"

"No, just when we found out he was killed in action and how I felt then."

Delia shrugged her shoulders. "It doesn't matter."

"Of course it does. I'll try harder."

Delia swallowed hard. "I appreciated all you did for me,

Clare. I couldn't have gotten through his death and the aftermath without you."

Which must have made their estrangement even harder. With that thought came pain behind her eyes. Briefly, she closed them and was able to will it away.

The coffee finished dripping. Delia poured them each a mug and brought both to the counter, where Clare reseated herself. Then Delia removed vanilla-flavored International Delight from the refrigerator and sat down. Clare picked up the bottle and poured some of the sweet liquid into her coffee.

"You knew that was for you?" Delia asked.

"Uh-huh. Do you want to talk more about Don?"

"No, I want to change the subject."

"Then, yes, I knew this was for me. Sometimes I just know things. It's all so odd."

"What does it feel like? Not remembering?"

"Very scary. And unsafe." She swallowed hard and massaged her temples. "When I try to remember, I get pain in my head. But some of what I recall since I came home yesterday is comforting. And smells trigger mostly good stuff."

"You have a lot to deal with."

"Especially alone."

"I don't know what I'd do without Donny."

"Your son." A flash of red hair and freckles filled her mind. "I remember what he looks like. Is he here?"

"No, every June when he gets out of school, he goes to stay with Don's parents for a while. I miss him, but it's good for them."

"Tell me about him."

Delia had her laughing out loud at the precocious seven-year-old's antics when the French doors to the kitchen opened.

"If this isn't a sight for sore eyes."

Delia smiled warmly at Brady. More warmly than she'd originally greeted Clare. "Isn't it? Just like old times."

Stepping inside, Brady kissed Delia on the cheek, then touched Clare's shoulder. He smelled even more familiar—she knew that cologne—making her lean toward him. He looked good, too, in jeans and a navy-blue shirt tucked in at the waist. Brady Langston kept in shape.

"Good morning. Are you all right?"

"Yes, I woke about eight. Delia was in the garden, and somehow we ended up here."

Delia had gone to the counter, poured another cup of coffee and added sugar. She served it to Brady and they exchanged a meaningful look. "Thanks, Dee."

Clare didn't have her memory back, but she knew certain things. Entering a house without knocking, a nickname, being served coffee without asking how it was taken and sharing pointed glances all indicated intimacy.

Apparently Delia and Brady had stayed close while Clare had grown apart from them. She wished she could remember why.

BRADY SAT AT THE DRAFTING table in his home office and stared at the walls, bookshelves and computer. On his desk sat the page proofs of one book to go over, and the beginning of another was in front of him. But right now, all he could think about was Clare.

After he found her at Delia's, they talked over coffee. Mostly she was comfortable, until something came up that she didn't remember. Then she'd get agitated and, worse, fearful. He couldn't stand watching her be afraid. After a while, he suggested a walk and she seemed to be itching for exercise. Why not? She'd never sat still for a minute before, even if she didn't remember that. Two long weeks in a hospital bed had decreased her strength and stamina but not her desire to move.

As they walked, she peppered him with questions about the Kramers, and he tried to fill her in the best he could. Don's death was still hard for him to talk about, even though he'd known the guy the shortest period of time. Brady had moved into the old house ten years ago when the others were all settled in. He soon came to love Don, like they did. And like Max and Clare, Brady had been devastated for a long time after their friend died.

Such grim thoughts often came these days when he was alone. He dragged himself up from the chair and walked into the living room. He'd insisted he and Clare leave their doors open in case she needed him. When he reached the front of his condo, he smiled at his own whimsy of creating the birds, which were supposed to represent the five of them. He fingered the goldfinch, Clare, who'd flown the coop. Shaking his head, he stepped into the hall. No sounds from her place. He went back to work, sat at the drafting table, and was just getting into Raoul the Rat and Millie the Mouse when the phone rang. Caller ID told him it was his agent, which was the only reason he answered.

"Brady? Hi, it's Leo."

"Hey, Leo."

"How's Clare doing?"

"Better. She's home. I'm on watch this afternoon, but she's sleeping, so guess where I am?"

"Please, tell me you're in your office."

"I am. And Millie and Raoul got one more page."

"Thank God. The publisher's breathing down my neck. They gave the extension, but begrudgingly."

"Thanks, Leo."

But what could they do anyway? Brady worked at his own pace and did things in his own time frame. It used to drive his workaholic ex-wife Gail crazy. He was successful though, and their marriage had struggled along a bumpy road until tragedy struck and Brady's whole life turned upside down.

"Did you hear me, Brady?"

Not exactly. His mind went where it always did these days. "Something about a delivery date."

"Funny."

"I don't know when it'll be done, Leo. I've promised to help out with Clare. I want to."

"You're in a perfect position to do that. You work at home, she's next door." A pause. "You sure there's nothing going on between you two other than friendship?"

He hesitated, then said, "Yeah, sure."

There was a knock on his open door, and then a "Yo…"

"Someone's here. I gotta go."

"Scan and e-mail me what you've done."

"You know I don't like to do that, Leo."

"It'll calm my nerves."

"Take a Valium." Max appeared at his door, and Brady motioned for him to wait.

"Come on. I need a Millie and Raoul fix."

"Maybe. Talk to you soon."

After he clicked off, he stood and faced his longtime friend, Max Mason, whom he'd known since high school, when they'd hung out together and avoided playing football. Max was big enough to compete, though, with the build of a linebacker. Brady had based a character on him once,

Mixy, the huge lovable rat. Max feigned outrage, but Brady had seen a few copies of the book on his buddy's shelf.

They hugged like men do—a bear clasp and pats on the back. Brady had always been grateful for Max's friendship, especially in the past year.

When he drew back, Max asked, "How is she?"

"She's home."

"I thought maybe. I saw the open door. I can help now. I got some time off."

"You did?"

"I said I'd help." He dropped his big form into the mahogany leather chair and propped his feet up on the ottoman.

"I know, but she's not your favorite person anymore."

His dark eyes narrowed and he ran a hand over his shaved head. Brady remembered when he'd worn it in an Afro. "No matter. If Dee and I don't help, you'll run yourself into the ground." He glanced at the desk. "Or worse, put aside your work again to help her."

Brady wasn't up for an argument, especially one they'd had so many times. "Want something?"

"No, I'm going to catch a nap. Long flight." Max was a pilot for a private company and had been flying his boss around the country while Clare lay in the hospital. "I won't say any more after this, but I gotta get one thing off my chest."

"Max…"

"I love you, bro. I don't want her to hurt you. Be careful and protect yourself."

"Point taken."

When Max left, Brady found it impossible to get back to his book. Again, he pushed away from the desk, got up and headed to Clare's condo. This time, he went in and found her in bed on her side, her hands under her face like she always slept. The pretty green sheet had slipped off, so he tucked it around her. His whole body responded to the sight of her, and the scent of her that permeated this room. Hell, this was all he needed now.

She looked so fragile, bruised and fearful, even in slumber. Her brow furrowed and she turned over fitfully. How on earth could Brady abandon her now?

Because she abandoned you. And Dee. And Max. Even her own sister.

He shook his head. It didn't matter. He had a Clare hex on him, and nothing could dispel it. He'd felt this way since the first day he met her...

"THE MEAL WAS TERRIFIC." Brady lazed back in his chair and spoke to Josie, the owner of Meloni's. This place was Max and Don and Delia's favorite restaurant, and his other cotenant in the house worked here. Having recently moved into the old Victorian, Brady had yet to meet Clare Boneli.

"Our assistant chef made it." The small, white-haired Italian woman smiled. "Which of course is why you're here." She picked up Brady's credit card—he insisted on paying—and smiled at his friends. "I'll be right back. Want something else?"

"Cappuccino would be nice," Don suggested. "Maybe the chef can join us."

"Sure. She's cleaned up already."

When Josie left, Brady asked, "That meal was something. Where did she learn to cook like this?"

Delia grinned like a proud mama. "After college, she went to culinary school, then she studied in France awhile."

She explained more about Clare's background until they heard, "Talking about me behind my back?"

Turning, Brady saw a slender blonde with eyes the color of grass carrying a tray of mugs.

"Yep, I'm filling Brady in."

Brady stood, took the tray and set it down. "You must be the chef." He held out his hand. "I'm the new tenant, Brady Langston."

Her grip was firm. "Clare Boneli."

They both took seats.

"Your Zucchini Boneli was wonderful."

"My grandmother's recipe." She motioned to the mugs she'd set on the table. "Drink up before your cappuccino gets cold. I poured myself one, too." She wore plain black pants that accentuated long legs and a white blouse that accentuated... He dragged his eyes to her face.

"Most of her recipes come from her extended Italian family," Delia said. "But she puts her own pizzazz in them."

A blush kissed Clare's cheeks. It was adorable.

Brady sipped his cappuccino. "The drink is different, too. What's in it?"

"A dash of nutmeg."

"Unusual. As was the zucchini. What's its secret?"

"Fresh zucchini, for one. I used to go out to the garden with Grandma and pick it. Couldn't let it get too big, though, or it would be tough."

"Did you spend a lot of time with your grandmother?"

"I lived with her." Real sadness filled her eyes. "My parents were killed in a car crash when I was ten. Grandma and Grandpa moved to America to take care of us. Grandma only died five years ago. I still feel her loss."

"I'm sorry." Brady cleared his throat. "My dad died

recently." The expression on her face was so empathetic, at that moment he felt a strong connection with her. "It's hard for me. But you were so little when your parents died. That must have been really tough."

"It was. Grandma Clarissa was wonderful, though. She taught me to cook."

"Her and culinary school and France."

Clare shook her head. "You have to stop bragging, Dee. Let Brady get to know me on his own."

"Finish telling me about the recipe."

"Along with extra sausage, I use cream and butter in the mixture."

He patted his stomach. "Oh, man, I'm going to have to work out extra hard tomorrow to stay in shape."

"Hmm. Maybe we can run together. I can't get Don or Max to go with me."

A huge grin. "I'd like that."

After they'd gotten back to the house and Max and the Kramers had gone to their respective places, Brady and Clare had talked long into the night. About their pasts. Their families. Their successes and failures.

She'd had big dreams then, as had he. They'd shared those, too. Who knew that, in the end, those dreams would pretty much destroy their relationship?

CHAPTER THREE

"THIS IS SILLY. I CAN'T EVEN go into my own kitchen?" Clare stood at the threshold of her bedroom, staring out at the hallway that led to the rest of the condo. After leaving Delia's, she and Brady had taken a walk, come back to the house, sat in the backyard and had lunch delivered. Then she'd come up to rest. Clare had fallen asleep just before Brady went to work in his home office. And now, at 4:00 p.m., she was restless. She sensed she wasn't used to inactivity. Hadn't she found sneakers and tennis shoes, along with a racket, in her closet? It was time she broached her own kitchen. She wanted to see her cookbooks. Get a glimpse of her old life.

Should she wait for Brady? He'd asked her to. Again she glanced at the hallway. Hell, she was thirty-six years old. She could go anywhere in her house if she wanted to. Besides, she had to start making her own decisions again. She knew in her heart it wasn't her style to let someone else do it for her.

Still, it was with tentative steps that she walked down the hall, through the living and dining rooms. When she reached the archway of the kitchen, she stopped and surveyed the area. Immediately a sense of well-being flooded her. *This* was Clare's space. She could feel it in her bones, her hands, even her breath. No longer afraid, she walked to the center island and smiled as she ran her hand over the granite countertop.

It was new, she realized. She'd remodeled in here, though she couldn't recall what the old kitchen was like. She took in the triple-bowled sink in the island, the built-in soap dispenser, Sub Zero refrigerator and two ovens.

There was a second smaller fridge under the counter. Pulling it open revealed a cold wine storage filled with several bottles.

We'll have the Romanée-Conti tonight, Clare. Brady had drawn out the several-hundred-dollar bottle. *Publishing your first cookbook is a big deal.*

Emboldened, she looked around for the books themselves. She caught sight of a display on a set of oak shelves on the far wall. When she got up close, she clapped her hand over her mouth. "Oh, good Lord, I don't believe it."

Face out were six cookbooks. All entitled *In Clarissa's Kitchen, Meals and Memories from Italy.* Her picture, with long hair, was on the cover of each. The first showed her in a casual dress, her hair down around her shoulders. Volumes two and three sported a similar pose. In four, though, her outfit was more sophisticated, and her hair was pulled back in a knot. Gracing the covers of the last two volumes were photos in different expensive outfits and more conservative hairdos.

What was that? Next to each of the cookbooks was a glossy version. Picking one up, she was hit with a flash of memory.

We got a coffee-table book contract, Clare. The publisher wants to do versions for display.

Whose voice was that? Jonathan's? No, she was sure it

wasn't. Who then? Was someone she worked with totally missing in her life now?

Feeling as if she were about to step off a cliff, she opened the cover. On the inside flap was *A Note from Clarissa.*

> Welcome to my world of cooking. On the pages that follow, though, you'll find much more. Accompanying the recipes are anecdotes from my childhood right through to today, letters to people who inspired me, and much more, all associated with my life and food. Mostly, they're a tribute to my grandma, Clarissa Boneli, who raised me. I hope you enjoy these great recipes and uplifting stories. *Mangia!*

Suddenly she realized she held a journal of sorts of her life. She swallowed hard and her hand tightened on the book. Should she read it? Would it be too much? She began to tremble—in anticipation or dread?

The decision was taken from her by a knock on the door Brady had asked her to leave ajar. He appeared in the archway. Still wearing the shorts and T-shirt he'd walked in, he looked concerned. "You're awake." He raised dark brows. "And came out here by yourself? I thought we agreed at lunch that you'd wait for me."

"No, that was your suggestion. I feel foolish, needing a babysitter, being afraid to go into my own kitchen." She sank back on a stool at the counter, clutching the cookbook to her chest. "When I came in here, and took out one of these, I felt good."

He smiled, said, "I'm glad to hear that," and joined her at the bar, dropping down on the stool next to her. Since waking up from the coma, she didn't like people crowding her, but when Brady stretched his legs out facing her, she braced her feet on the bottom rung of his stool. He nodded to the book, and his blue eyes sparkled like sapphires. "You should be proud of those. You're a big success."

She smiled back at him, wanting to know more about him. "What about you? Are you a success? I don't even know what you do."

For a minute, he looked puzzled. "I'm an artist. Actually, an illustrator."

It was like getting hit with a blast of cold water. "Oh, the sketches in the hallway? They're yours. I had a visceral response when I saw them. Brady, they're terrific."

"You were the one who insisted they be mounted and hung out there. You had them framed even before I said yes."

"Where'd I get them?"

"Um, mostly from the books I've published."

"You publish books, too? Which ones? How many? Can I see something else you've done?"

His gaze dropped to her chest. "You're holding one."

"Huh?"

"Turn the book over, Clare."

She tensed, afraid for the first time since she'd come into this room. She stared at him warily.

"Go ahead. It won't hurt you. It's a good memory."

She turned the book around.

On the back was his picture. Dressed less formally than she, he wore pressed jeans, a silk T-shirt and a taupe blazer. His hair was a bit shorter, but his eyes were the same, long-lashed, crystalline-blue. She read the note with his picture, then peered over at him. "You illustrated my cookbooks?"

"Uh-huh. The anecdotes you wrote and my illustrations are what set them apart from all the other gazillion cookbooks on the market." He hesitated. "We have a new one in the works, too."

She found herself pleased at what he told her and wanted to know more. "I have a cooking show, too. Are you part of that?"

His expression darkened. "I've been a guest. Your viewers wrote in that they liked it when I was there."

Though she couldn't recall any of what he was telling her, she could imagine someone with his good looks and apparent charm would be a hit with women watching the show.

But he didn't seem too happy about this. "Are you still on the show?"

He shook his head. "Clare, you don't remember anything about this?"

"No."

A deep frown creased his forehead.

"Why aren't you on the show anymore?"

Not answering, he stood and went to the fridge. Pulling out a beer, he uncapped it and took a long swig. She watched his throat work and felt something…warm inside her. He set the beer down on the counter and stood across from her, his hands braced on the granite.

"Your boss, Jonathan, wanted the show…scaled up, you might say. A scruffy artist hanging around in a state-of-the-art kitchen didn't hit the target audience he wanted."

Her eyes widened. "Oh my God, did I call you a scruffy artist?"

"No! He did."

She struggled to remember. Instead, images of snakes clouded her mind, just like in the dream. Her temples hurt again. "I don't remember any of it."

He didn't say more, just watched her. Hurt clouded his eyes.

"Why didn't I stand up to him?"

"Ah, the sixty-four thousand-dollar question." Before she could respond, he asked, "Do you remember anything about…our relationship?"

She nodded. "Yes, good things. I had flashes as soon as I came home yesterday—cooking for you, you carrying up grocery bags, helping with the garden."

"Those are early memories."

"From how long ago?"

"About eight or nine years."

"My therapist told me that research says those memories often return first. The ones closest to the event that caused the amnesia—if it is psychological—come back last."

"Yes." He appeared embarrassed. "I read that on the Internet."

"The memories that aren't coming back? Those are the times when I hurt you, aren't they?"

"I didn't say that, Clare."

"You didn't have to. And it isn't only you. Delia, too. My own sister doesn't even call much."

"Cathy's sensitive where you're concerned, ever since you were little and your parents died. But she loves you, Clare, and she's coming as soon as she gets back from Europe. You'll have a great reunion."

"Still. It's so odd feeling good things for all of you and…them not being returned."

"They are returned. We've just had a rough time of it lately."

Standing, she circled around the bar and approached

him. This close, she could see the nick from shaving he must have gotten this morning. His chest rose and fell, and his features were taut. "Brady, I'm sorry that I've hurt you in the past. I sense we were really close."

"We were." His voice was husky, calling forth a memory that fled before it fully formed.

Suddenly she wanted this man to hold her again, like he had when he'd carried her last night. So she moved into him and slid her arms around his waist. As natural as spring rain, his arms encompassed her. His sigh matched hers. Closing her eyes, she placed her head on his heart.

Though she didn't remember what she'd done, it was obvious she'd hurt this heart of his. The thought shamed her.

"How is it going at home?" Anna Summers, Clare's psychotherapist, smiled over at her from where she sat on a stuffed chair in her hospital office. Clare had taken a similar chair opposite her in the cheery space—sand-colored walls, nice Berber carpet, wooden accents. She felt good in here, too, and had been more than willing to come back on this Wednesday morning.

"It's better than being in the hospital. Some of my memory's come back." She told Anna about the flashes she'd had about Brady, Delia and Don, Max and cooking.

"Interesting. They're all about the people from the house." She cocked her head. "None about Jonathan?"

"I hadn't thought of it that way. Maybe because he had to go away and the others are around all the time. I've talked to him every day on the phone but, truthfully, the conversations are strained. It's hard enough facing people you don't know in person."

"Maybe it's his absence. But you've known him the

shortest time. Remember, with retrograde amnesia, the earlier memories come back first."

"I was just talking to Brady about that."

Anna crossed her legs and adjusted the skirt of her beige suit. "How does it feel to be in your house?"

"What do you mean?"

"Is it like sleeping in a stranger's bed? Like you're wearing someone else's clothes?"

"Not at all. I sense everything's mine. I chose something to wear this morning without fretting about it and felt immediately at home in the kitchen."

"It's good that everything isn't foreign."

"I guess. But other things aren't so good."

"Like?"

Clare fidgeted with the bracelet she'd put on with khaki pants and a yellow blouse. "I've found some other things out about my life. About me. Some bad things."

"From these flashes of memories?"

"No, those were all good. But the tension among Max, Delia and me became obvious right away. So I asked about it." She told Anna that she'd grown away from her group of friends. "The problem is I don't feel that way about them now. I'm sad that they're so wary and I want to be closer to them." She thought for a minute. "Anna, do personalities change when someone has amnesia?"

"Sometimes. Especially in cases of permanent amnesia. There's a movie called *Regarding Henry* where Harrison Ford gets shot and turns into a totally different person than he was before the incident. He never regains his memory, though, and he retains the new personality."

"So I could just stay the person I am now?"

"Maybe. But keep in mind, you won't do anything with amnesia that you wouldn't normally do. That often comforts people who are afraid they'll do negative things. But in your case, who you are now is the real Clare, too."

She frowned. "But I could turn back into who I was right before the accident?"

"Perhaps. We've discussed how nebulous this malady is. But here's another way to look at it. You can make any changes in your life that you want. You're in control of that with or without your memory."

Clare stared at Anna. "I wonder if I'll still want to be close to them when my memory returns." The thought made her incredibly sad.

"Take one day at a time." Anna held her gaze. "What about Brady? He was at the hospital every day, too. And you seemed to gravitate toward him. Is there any tension between you two?"

"No. Just warmth. A lot of it. And security. I feel safe with him." She crooked a shoulder. "Safer than with Jonathan."

"You and Brady were close for a longer period of time."

"Maybe. It feels like more than that, though."

Anna leaned forward. "Go with your gut, Clare. Act on the instinct that remembers things for you. A good deal of research into what's known as cellular memory shows our cells store memories. I support that theory. Have you seen those movies about body-part transplants, where the recipient acquires the memories and experiences of the donor and often gets flashes of that person's life? You could and probably do have residual memories of everything that's happened to you built right into your cell structure."

"That's something to consider."

"Anything else about Jonathan or Brady?"

"One thing. Obviously, Jonathan and I were close—physically. How could I forget being intimate with a man, Anna?"

"There have been documented cases of people forgetting a spouse and even a child, Clare." Anna frowned. "He's not asking for intimacy, is he?"

"No, not yet. No, he wouldn't do something like that. He's been selfless in this whole thing."

"Then bide your time and see how you feel about it all. You've only been home a few days."

"Sounds like a plan."

"Now let's talk about your dreams. Though I'm not into symbol hunting, they're a crucial part of amnesia and should be discussed."

A chill ran through Clare, and she rubbed her arms as she recalled Monday night's dream. "I'm still having nightmares."

"Most amnesiacs do."

"I can't remember them all, but Monday's stays with me. Brady and Jonathan were snakes. One bit me, and one curled around my wrists."

"Hmm. Who did what?"

Clare told her. "Do you think it's significant?"

"As I explained right after you woke up, dreams are a person's unconscious asserting itself, even if that person doesn't have amnesia. I'd like you to write down the dreams you do remember. In as much detail as possible."

Clare nodded.

"Is there anything else you'd like to talk about today?"

"Yes. I'm going stir-crazy."

"You've only been home two days."

"I was in the hospital two weeks. I need to do more than I'm doing."

Anna smiled. "Then do it."

"I've been walking, but I found tennis stuff in the closet. Am I ready to play?"

"If you think you are."

"And I'd like to drive again."

The therapist looked thoughtful. "Can you do that?"

"I don't know. I haven't tried."

"How did you get here?"

"Brady. He's been a doll about all this. He's waiting outside."

Anna watched her. "Your whole face lights up when you talk about him."

"Does it? How odd, when I'm…involved with Jonathan."

"Something to think about. Be careful with the driving. You don't have procedural amnesia. You seem to know how to do things. But test-drive with someone in the car for a while. Don't go alone for a week or so. Especially with the headaches."

"All right." Clare shook her head. "It's all so frustrating."

"I'll bet. But your memory is starting to come back. You're making terrific progress."

It didn't feel that way. And Clare worried about things. "Anna, do you think some traumatic event caused my amnesia?"

"You had severe head trauma. But your last tests indicated there's no brain swelling now, and no apparent damage. However, why you were out at 2:00 a.m. on that road and what led up to it is missing from your mind, and that is significant. So, to answer your question, I believe it very well could be psychological."

"I almost don't want to remember."

"Clare, if your amnesia is psychological, you *don't* want to remember. But you most likely will. And you should prepare yourself for that."

They made an appointment for the following week, Anna wished her well and Clare went to find Brady. She was unnerved by her talk with the counselor and needed to see him to calm down. That he could do that for her was another mystery.

He was waiting outside the office, though she'd told him to go get coffee or something to eat. He stood when he saw her. The worry on his face made her give him a smile.

"Hey, how'd it go?"

"Fine."

"You're lying. I can see it in your expression."

"It's hard, articulating all my fears."

"Man, I bet it is." He slid an arm around her and leaned in close. "You know, you can talk to me about those fears. We used to stay up late and share everything we were afraid of in life. Takes the sting out of them."

"It sounds like we spent a lot of time together."

"We did. After I moved in, Don was still alive and Max was working for a commercial airline, so he wasn't home much. In some ways it was just you and me, babe."

And that had changed. Poor Brady. She wondered if she could ever make it up to him.

SEATED ACROSS THE TABLE from his longtime friend, Mitch Anderson, Jonathan felt better than he had earlier when he couldn't reach Clarissa. He and Mitch had gone to boarding school together and seen each other through a lot of scrapes. Sometimes Jonathan missed the boy he used to be—more carefree, more spontaneous. He definitely missed Mitch, who'd met him here at the restaurant in the Hyatt hotel where Jonathan was staying in Chicago.

"So, how'd the Chef's Delight thing go? Their stocks are sky-high." Mitch was an investment broker and followed the market daily. Jonathan used to take more of an interest in stocks than he did now. Of course, lately, he'd had a lot on his mind.

He told Mitch, "Clarissa's going to be getting some of those options."

"Really? Wow." Mitch lazed back in the chair and sipped the merlot they'd ordered. "You struck quite a deal, then."

"Well, I had to fly out our lawyers." That had kept him here an extra day. "But they hammered out a lucrative contract for both the station and Clarissa herself."

"No offense, but...for a local show?"

"They recognize, as do I, that she'll syndicate soon." He told his friend of his plans for the Cooking Channel.

Mitch raised his glass. "Congratulations. You've brought her into the limelight and now, so to speak, her star is shining."

"I hope she doesn't leave me in the dust."

Mitch burst out laughing. He had a big belly laugh that contrasted with his polished good looks. "You can't mean that. Rockford's Most Eligible Bachelor?"

The designation a local magazine had given Jonathan had embarrassed him, though originally it had brought him plenty of dates. But once he met Clarissa, that part of his life was over. "I'm in love, Mitch. I don't want anyone else."

Immediately Mitch sobered. "I didn't realize things between you and Clarissa were that serious. Since your divorce, I haven't heard you talk like this."

Jonathan had been married for six years to a nice woman he'd met at his country club. His parents hadn't been happy when they'd divorced, but Marilyn and he both knew there was no spark there. Thankfully, they'd parted friends.

The feelings he'd had for his ex were nothing close to what he felt for Clarissa. He sighed, thinking of the forced celibacy her illness had brought about. He missed her body as much as her mind.

"Jonathan, you're scowling. Do you have reason to think Clarissa is going to leave you?"

Filling Mitch in on the whole sad story of Clarissa's amnesia made Jonathan feel even worse.

"Why didn't you say something before this? You only see those things on TV. I don't know that I've ever been privy to a real-life case. It's a remarkable story."

"It's a nightmare. She loved me, I know she did, and now she doesn't even remember me. Nothing."

Mitch set his wine down and leaned forward. "Does she have any memories of anybody?"

"She didn't in the hospital, but who knows now? She lives in a condo in this old Victorian house. The other three people who own there were her close friends until I came along."

"And?"

"She grew apart from them. Was on the verge of moving out and in with me. Then she had the accident."

"What caused it?"

He shrugged. He'd never lied outright to Mitch, but now he'd skirt the truth somewhat. "Nobody really knows. She left her condo and went out into the rainy night, cracked up her car."

The waitress came and took their orders. After she left,

Jonathan said, "Let's table this conversation. It's depressing to think about her accident."

"Whatever you want."

"So tell me about those two kids of yours." It seemed impossible, but at only forty Mitch had two teenagers.

"They're making me crazy. Wait until you have your own. I'm teaching Nicky to drive. Talk about nightmares."

The rest of the evening was pleasant, and when he went back to his room, Jonathan was thinking about having his own kids, teaching them to drive, proudly showing pictures as Mitch had. He sat on the divan, took out his cell and punched in Clarissa's number.

She answered on the fourth ring. "Hello."

His mood lightened at the sound of her voice. "Hi, honey. It's me."

No response.

Damn it, didn't she even recognize his voice? "Jonathan."

"Yes, hi. How's Chicago?"

"I've had a successful trip. But I miss you."

Please say you miss me, too.

"Successful?"

"We got the contract."

"Is that good?"

"Very. I'll explain the details when I get back."

"When will that be?"

"Friday night. I've made reservations at your favorite restaurant."

A long hesitation. "Oh, good." He heard another sound.

"Was that a yawn? Are you getting enough sleep?"

"Uh-huh. I'm in bed right now. I was watching TV."

"Do you remember any shows?" He hadn't thought of this side of amnesia—would she recognize songs, shows, films?

"A couple brought flashbacks."

"Any of me? We used to watch *Law and Order* together."

"Um, no, but I'll make sure I catch an episode and see what happens."

He tried to keep the frustration out of his voice. This wasn't her fault, but he could curse fate for what had happened. "Honey, it'll come back. Don't worry."

"I know."

"Go to sleep." He waited. "And dream of me."

When she hung up, he stretched out on the couch and stared up at the ceiling. He'd meant it when he'd told Mitch that he had never loved anyone like he loved Clarissa. And it had been going so well. Still, he hadn't lost yet.

As he lay there, he convinced himself that as soon as he got back to Rockford, she'd start remembering him. When that possibility began to worry him—there were definitely some things he didn't want her to remember yet—he pushed them out of his mind.

All would be well as soon as they could spend some quality time together.

It would. It would!

CHAPTER FOUR

WITH THE LATE-MORNING sun beating down on them, Brady stood behind Clare, one hand at her waist, the other on her arm. Man, it felt good to touch her again. Too good. His whole body responded to her nearness. "Adjust your hips to the left," he said rather hoarsely. "That's it. Now, turn your grip about forty-five degrees on the racket's handle. Good. That's how you hit your backhand."

They'd been reviewing the mechanics of tennis, and she seemed to remember them with only one demonstration. "Got it."

Reluctantly he backed away, but he didn't move to the other side of the court. "I still don't think this is a good idea."

"Dr. Summers said I could play if we took it easy."

"She told you that yesterday morning. I'm not sure she meant for you to run right out and do it."

Rays of sun caught her hair, turning its blond strands lighter. He knew how silky it would feel if he ran his hands through it.

"Brady, you're sweet to be concerned, but this is my fourth day home, and I'm dying for more exercise."

"I'll hit you some shots, but take it easy."

He'd gotten a cage full of bright green balls from the clubhouse at Midtown Tennis, and they'd gone outside, forgoing the indoor courts. He knew she'd been playing at Harris's swank country club, a place she didn't recall, so he didn't remind her. If only the rest were that easy.

From the other side of the net, she smiled over at him. "Thanks, Brady. For this and everything."

"You're welcome. I snapped my Achilles tendon four years ago playing basketball, and you were a huge help. So I'm returning the favor."

She stared at him, trancelike. "You were a big baby about it."

"I was not!" His eyes narrowed when he saw the gleam in hers. "You don't really remember, do you? You're making that up."

"Gotcha."

He laughed out loud as he took his position. "Ready?"

"I hope so."

He hit a weak one over the net. She returned it easily. Three more followed in the same vein.

She bounced the ball in front of her a few times, which used to be her habit when they'd played together. "This is boring, isn't it?"

"We usually play harder."

"Let's put at least a little more behind the hits."

They continued to lob the ball back and forth, using more oomph each time.

At a pause in the volleying, she asked, "Who wins, Brady, when we *really* play?"

"I do, of course."

She gave him a sideways glance. "You're lying. I'll bet I'm better than you."

"Are you remembering that?"

"No."

"Then, nope, I'm the better player."

This time she laughed out loud, which hadn't happened much since the accident. Laughter and pure fun had been a routine part of their lives together until Harris had come along. Snagging the next ball with her hand, she headed to the back of the court.

"That outfit looks great on you," he called from behind her. It did, too, and made his mouth water. And it felt good to flirt with her again. This also had been part of their history—the innocent, suggestive remarks that made them both smile. Though for him, things between them had been far less innocent long before the accident.

She glanced down at the white skirt and red halter top she wore. When she pivoted back around, she gave him a haughty look. "You're just trying to distract me."

Huh. She was distracting *him*, big-time. "I don't need to. I told you I always win."

Stopping at the serve line, she faced him. "Let's play a game."

"I'm not—"

"I'll take it easy, I promise."

Without his instruction, the mechanics of the serve were there for her: throw the ball up, racket angled behind down her back, over her head, slam! During the course of the serve, her top pulled up and Brady got a very nice glimpse of a tanned patch of skin on her midriff. Arrgh!

He barely reached the ball in time because of his double take on her stomach, but he managed to hit it back. She raced forward and sent it soaring over the net. He didn't even try to get to the shot.

Her hands went to her hips. "You missed that on purpose."

"I did. I don't want you playing too hard."

"I won't, but I gotta move. I need exercise, I need to sweat."

He opened his mouth but bit back a sexual innuendo. Those were better left unsaid right now. "Maybe a little."

She served three more times and won the game. "Told you I was good," she gloated.

He grinned. "My serve."

He let her win a few points, but took the last three of the next game. She was running around—and sweating—and breathing hard. "God, this feels good."

On another volley, she charged the net to return his short lob. Brady hit it back way over her head. She raced toward the ball and was just about there when she stumbled and went down. "Ohh…"

Leaping the net, he was at her side in seconds and knelt down. "Damn it, what was I thinking?"

"I twisted my ankle a bit. It doesn't hurt much." She rubbed her foot. "I'm sorry I pushed. Probably too hard." She shrugged her shoulder. "But it felt good."

Chuckling, he reached for her foot. Very gently, he untied her sneaker, removed it and her sock. He palpated her sole, her ankle and her shin. "Hurt?"

She sighed. "No, it feels good."

"The injury feels good?"

"It isn't injured. Your fondling me feels good."

Oh, Lord, now *she* was flirting.

"I was not fondling!" A smile quirked at his lips. "I was checking for damage." He glanced around. "We're done here."

"I guess." After sliding her sock and shoe on, he stood and offered her his hand. "Here, let me help you up."

She took the assistance. When he didn't let go after she

was on her feet, she moved in close to him. His arms slid around her as if he'd never stopped hugging her. His whole body tightened. "You okay? Dizzy?"

"No. I like it when you hold me. I feel safe. We must be really close."

He had to clear his throat. "We are."

She drew back. "Thanks."

"Time for a nap?"

"Not on your life. I'm so tired of sleeping." Her eyes sparkled like the old Clare's. "I know. Let's go to the grocery store."

He grabbed the cage and started picking up balls. "I wondered when that would kick in."

"What?"

"The grocery store's your favorite place."

"You think it would be okay to go there, or would it push my memory too much?"

"I think it'd be okay. Let's finish up here, and we'll head over."

They pulled up to Weidman's fifteen minutes later. Clare had hoped for a bit of recognition at the sight of the big blue sign on the huge storefront, but none came. Brady squeezed her hand and held it after they exited his Blazer. Once inside, he got a cart and set it in front of her.

"Where to?" she asked.

"You tell me."

"Hmm. I'll wander."

First she went to the dairy counter and selected goat cheese. Then she headed to the vegetable department. They strolled along, and Clare seemed to absorb the sounds and sights and smells of her surroundings. She picked up onions and juicy tomatoes. Bypassing the bagged kind, she chose curly red lettuce in a bunch. They kept going: chicken, canned artichokes. By the time she snagged a couple of loaves of fresh bread, she turned to him. "I have the ingredients for a chicken artichoke dish I used to make." Her face lit, and she smiled broadly. "Oh, wow."

"You remember."

"Yes, suddenly." She closed her eyes. "There's more."

"What?"

"Me behind a counter, facing cameras, wearing a pretty fuchsia apron with embroidery on the front of it." She looked at him. "I made this dish in one of my cooking shows, didn't I?"

"Yeah, one of the first demos you did."

"Do you like this recipe?"

"A lot."

"Will Max and Delia come if I cook tonight, do you think?"

"If they're free."

But he wasn't so sure of his statement. Max and Delia had each stayed with her a couple of times, Max overseeing mostly when she was sleeping. He knew Delia had brought over a photo album and showed her pictures of their life together. Clare had laughed at the way she looked in college, made jokes at the images of herself surrounded by boxes on moving day, and got tears in her eyes over the baby pictures of Donny, whom she'd helped raise. But there was still an underlying tension among them all.

When she and Brady reached the checkout line, something else occurred to her. "Do I have tapes of the shows, Brady?"

"Uh-huh, from the studio."

"I'd like to watch this one, then make the meal."

Without speaking, he paid the cashier. He had a bad feeling about her watching the show that had, in the long run, taken her away from him.

"I'll stop if I get a headache or upset."

"I don't think you should rush your memory."

"I won't."

Though he was worried about this step, he was pleased about one thing. Over the course of the past few days, she'd taken to asking his opinion, his permission sometimes, like she used to in the old days. It had gone both ways and they'd spent a lot of years consulting each other on choices and decisions to be made. It was only right that she should now, after what they'd meant to each other.

When they got back to her place, Brady found the show's CDs packed away in a cabinet and stuck the one she wanted, labeled by the meal, in the player. Sitting next to her on the couch, he watched as she came on and smiled out at the camera.

Now memories flooded *him*—her nervousness the night before, him calming her down. That day, they'd all been over the moon about it. He, Delia and Max were almost as excited as she was and had come to the studio for the first taping. She'd looked great, too; he'd given her that apron with the name of the show stitched on the front.

"Oh!" she said, seated next to him. "The music is familiar. It's *familiar.*"

Lord, was this going to bring everything back? Was he ready for that? "Maybe it's too soon."

"No, it feels right." Her eyes widened as she stared at the screen. "My hair…" She touched her own short curls. "I look good with it long."

"You look good with it short, too. And if you don't like the style now, your hair grows fast."

Mesmerized, she stared at the TV. So did he.

"WELCOME TO *CLARISSA'S KITCHEN*. Today we're going to make Chicken Rosie, a recipe my great-aunt taught me." She laughed and the camera panned in on her, capturing the amused twinkle in her beautiful green eyes. "Aunt Rosie didn't work in amounts. This recipe came to me orally, in directions that read a package of chicken, some tomatoes, artichokes if you can find them..."

AS SHE SPOKE, she chatted about her grandmother's sister, whom Brady had never met. But he knew that she was big and round, with white hair and a huge smile.

"I'M GOING TO BROWN the chicken, but not too much." Grease sizzled in the pan. "Don't make the mistake of letting it get too done, because it'll cook more when everything's combined. Meanwhile chop up the onions, tomatoes, olives and broccoli."

She picked up a jar of tomato sauce. "This is my homemade sauce, canned early this year, but you can use grocery store sauce if you want."

"YUCK," CLARE SAID ALOUD in the living room. She had a very familiar look on her face.

Brady laughed. "You remember you were a purist, huh?"

"I guess. I'd never eat sauce from a jar."

"No, you wouldn't."

She glanced at him as a commercial came on. "Was I a snob?"

"About food you were."

"Just that?"

He hesitated.

She put the CD on Pause. "Brady, I've pieced together that I worked too much. And I wasn't close to people anymore, like Delia and Max. And obviously you." She nodded to the screen. "Was I that way when the show started?"

"Not when it started. The four of us were best friends and did a lot together."

"Like what?"

"We played cards in a euchre group and we socialized with the other players. We had a bowling team. A dinner group."

"Hmm. How sad that we stopped that."

He nodded to the CD, wanting to get out of this discussion. "Let's get you back on."

The rest of the half hour distracted her. She had no memories until the closing music. Then she said, "Oh!"

"What?"

She turned to him. "You and Max and Delia were there backstage. With flowers and champagne." She closed her eyes. "Damn, there's nothing more."

He was glad she had no recollection of the aftermath because Jonathan Harris had horned in, and Brady had gotten angry about how the guy usurped their celebration.

"What happened? You're scowling."

"I guess I'm worried this is too much. Did you enjoy the show?"

"Very much. I'm tired, though."

"You don't have to cook, Clare."

She stood. "I want to. I'll sleep, then I'm making the meal. You'll call the others?"

"Yeah."

"I hope they can come."

"Me, too."

"It'll be like old times."

Hardly, Brady thought, wondering if he'd made a mistake by getting her hopes up about Delia's and Max's presence. At one time, they'd refused to let Clare cook for them ever again.

AWAKE AND RESTED, CLARE HEADED to her kitchen with a smile on her face. She'd showered and put on a loose-fitting cotton dress that seemed appropriate to cook in. At the bookshelf, she picked up the first cookbook and crossed to the counter. She'd watched the tape but hadn't memorized the recipe, so she propped it open on a beautiful teak book holder, and began to assemble the dinner.

First she got out the chicken and browned it. As the smell wafted up to her, she remembered something.

Clare, girl, we just love it when you're testing new recipes.

Honest, Clare, this one is my fave.

The voices belonged to Max and Delia. She saw vague outlines of them sitting at her kitchen counter as she cooked for them. And she knew it wasn't the first time they'd been there. Suddenly, she knew she used to try out her recipes on them, and they'd give her honest feedback. The feelings elicited by the memory were all positive—warm, deep friendship. Intellectually, she'd known they used to be really close, but now she actually *recalled* it.

But they weren't anymore. She shook her head, ludicrously regretting that had happened even though she couldn't remember why. Maybe she could start to rectify that tonight.

She turned on the radio built into the wall. Fiddling with the tuner, she found a station she liked then returned to cooking. The process was soothing and surprisingly mind-blanking. There was something rhythmic about it, something fluid, and it made her feel "right in her skin," as Grandma Boneli used to say.

Grandma Boneli—the woman who raised her when her parents died. Again, Clare closed her eyes and tried to focus. Soon the image came to her. It was the one from the dream she'd had: a tall, sturdily built woman in a house-dress, hair completely white and a smile the size of Sicily. Warmth seeped into her. She felt loved and cared for.

She continued to cook, humming along with the radio, remembering the melodies. They were golden oldies, from the sixties and seventies. They made her smile…and sent her reeling into a flashback…

"Come on, girl, join in." Max was dancing with Delia and cutting a pretty mean rug, though it was on the kitchen tile. *Her* kitchen tile.

"I have to finish dinner."

Brady, who'd been reading the newspaper at the counter, stood and grabbed her around the waist. "That can wait. Never be too busy to dance."

She laughed and fell into a jitterbug with him, then they switched partners for the next song and she and Max did the salsa…step, step, quick step, step, step… She was laughing hysterically at the flubs she made and the teasing Max tossed her way.

SHE WAS DRAWN FROM the pleasant memory when she heard Brady call out from the front of the house, "We're here."

The clock said it was 6:00 p.m.; they were right on time. The three of them entered the kitchen, but instead of the camaraderie from her memories of earlier times, Max, Delia and even Brady all radiated anxiety.

"What's wrong?" she asked.

Max spoke. "Been a long time since we did this, Clare."

Brady said, "Max…"

"No, let him speak." Clare wiped her hands on her apron and faced the big man squarely. Instead of fear, she felt…sorrow. "Every time you've been here—and you, too, Delia, to a degree—it's been strained between us. The problem for me is that the memories I have of you two are good. As a matter of fact, I just remembered all of us dancing in the kitchen."

Delia came forward. "I know, Clare. We have those good ones, too."

"But too many bad ones to compensate?"

Delia shook her head. "Not for me."

"Jury's still out for me." Max walked to her fridge, got out a bottle of wine and was pouring it before he stilled. "I forgot. I used to help myself all the time. Is it okay?"

"Of course it is. I like the familiarity you all have with my home. Helping yourself to things in the kitchen, coming in without knocking."

"We used to." Max's expression was stern.

Crossing to him, she touched his arm and got another flash. *The two of them, out back in the garden, planting. He was talking about Stephanie. Another image, of a beautiful girl with caramel skin and gorgeous hair.* "Who's Stephanie?"

He cocked his head, surprised. "My daughter."

"Are you married?"

There was genuine emotion in his eyes, and Clare realized he was a man who felt things deeply but didn't always show it. "No. I didn't even know I had a daughter until about seven years ago. She found me on the Internet."

"She's a bright, interesting girl," Clare said.

"How do you know?"

"I just do. I must have seen her, spent some time with her."

"You did." Max cleared his throat. "You taught her to cook on her visits here."

"Isn't that a pleasant memory, Max?"

He cleared his throat. "Yeah, I guess. She, um, asks about you all the time."

"We'll have to catch up the next time she visits."

"So," Brady asked, picking up the wine bottle and pouring glasses for him, Delia and Clare. "Shall we toast?"

Clare smiled and lifted her glass. This, too, was familiar. "To new beginnings."

Max hesitated, but finally clinked glasses with her. When she looked over, she saw that Delia had tears in her eyes. Brady's stance was stiff, as if he was holding emotion in. Holy hell, how had things gone so wrong with these wonderful people?

Suddenly, Clare wasn't so anxious to get her memory back.

CHAPTER FIVE

ROONEY'S WAS ONE of the most popular restaurants in Rockford. Its wooden decor was sophisticated, not rustic, and pristine white linen tablecloths along with the low hum of a string quartet in the background created a chic ambience. On Jonathan's first night back—Friday—he'd picked the spot for dinner with Clarissa.

"This place is lovely, Jonathan. Thanks for bringing me here." She didn't sound like she meant it, though. She seemed more distant than she'd been when he left on Monday. Damn it, he wished he hadn't had to go away and leave her. He needed to keep her connected to him, for his sake and hers.

"Maybe tonight will jog more pleasant memories."

She sipped the club soda she'd ordered. "Do we come here often?"

"Yes, it's one of your favorite restaurants."

She smiled. Her color was good, and the rosy tinges of her cheeks were highlighted by the soft silk of her peach suit. Jonathan loved how she looked and appreciated the fact that he never had to worry that she'd turn up dressed inappropriately for one of their nights out. When he entertained clients and prospective sponsors, she was a gracious hostess.

Reaching across the table, he took her hand. She stiffened a minute, then relaxed and rested her palm in his.

"I'm sorry I had to be gone these four days. I wish I could have taken time off and been with you."

"You missed work all those days when I was in the hospital. I told you it was all right. Besides," she said, drawing back her hand, "I had plenty of company."

Exactly what worried him.

"Is your memory coming back?" They'd discussed this briefly on the phone but not again since he'd returned. He'd gone right over to get her after his plane had landed, and on the short drive to the restaurant, they'd talked about the deal he'd made with the Chef's Delight people.

"In bursts and flashes. Sometimes I see images, sometimes I feel things. Then there are full-blown flashbacks, where even small details are there."

"Anything significant?" He smiled at her. "Anything about me?"

"Ah, no. About my friends. Jonathan, I told you on the phone, that's probably because I've been with them and not you."

She'd been with him daily in the hospital but still didn't remember him. "Perhaps."

"I'm sure now that you're back I'll remember…us."

"I hope so, Clarissa."

Delicate little lines formed on her brow. "Why do you call me that and the others call me Clare?"

"Because when I met you, it was through *Clarissa's Kitchen*. I never knew you by your nickname." He cleared his throat, feeling anger sour his stomach. "Your friends think it's pretentious, my calling you that, but to me you've always been Clarissa."

"I think it's sweet." She frowned. "Jonathan, Brady and

Max and Delia said I got busy with work. Too busy for them, or anything else."

"That's not true. You did a lot of things, good ones, for the community."

"Like what?"

"We arranged to have the food you cooked at the station brought to the nursing home across the street, and sent more meals over when you were trying out recipes. You also did cooking demonstrations there. The older folks loved it."

"I did?" Her face glowed. "Because I was close to Grandma Boneli, right?"

"Partly. But you have an affinity for older people. As do I. We have that in common." He smiled. "One of my most pleasant experiences as a child was staying with my grandparents on summer vacations. I adored them, especially my grandfather."

"That's nice."

"You also gave money to soup kitchens in town."

Her eyes widened. "Oh. I used to work at one. Downtown. With a lot of hungry people and cooks who fed them."

Damn, she remembered that and not him! "Yes. But that was one thing you had to stop because of the show and the demand for your cookbooks."

Again, she frowned. "I wonder if I could go work there now, even if I don't have my memory back. Surely I can serve food or cook for people again."

"Let's wait until we see the doctor."

"I already did, Jonathan. On Wednesday."

"I wish you'd changed that appointment so I could have gone with you. Talked to the doctor myself."

"Brady thought it was a good idea to keep it. He drove me there."

Of course he did. "I see. What did Dr. Summers say?"

"She told me I could do what I wanted within reason. Not to push too much with things like driving. But I played tennis, and it felt great."

"Tennis?" Their game. "Let me guess. With Langston."

"Yes. Jonathan—"

Frowning, he picked up the leather binder. "Want to look at the menu?"

Probably sensing his pique, she gave him a strained smile. She was right, too. While he'd been away, he'd thought long and hard about the situation and promised himself he'd stay cool through all this, not pressure her, and most of all not come down on her about Langston. Then the first mention of what they'd done together while he'd been gone had set Jonathan off.

"Everything's good here," he said in a more placating tone.

"Think I'll know what I like?" she asked.

"Good question. I could tell you."

"No, let me see." She opened the red leather booklet and began to read aloud. "Mussels, escargot. Plantain shrimp. Salmon with artichokes and feta cheese over spinach. Hmm. Chocolate bombe." Carefully, she studied the ingredients of each dish. "I'm surprised they put saffron in the chicken."

He chuckled.

"What? Oh, I've said that before?"

"Yeah, critique the menu, and we'll see if you're true to form."

It was fun, listening to her comments, which were right on target with what she thought before the accident. He settled some. Maybe she would evolve into the old Clarissa, with or without her memory. He wanted the woman back who loved him, valued him in her life.

"Now, the true test. What are you going to order?"

Staring at the menu, she said, "I'll have the Blue Point oysters, the iceberg lettuce and blue cheese salad, and the mahi-mahi." She looked up. "How'd I do?"

"Good choice. You've ordered exactly that before."

"When before?"

He picked a pleasant time to recount. "On your last birthday. We went out to dinner here."

"September 17. Brady told me."

Her hand went to her neck; Jonathan smiled broadly and nodded at the diamond pendant she'd put on. "That was a present from me last year."

She clasped the single jewel in her palm. "It's breathtaking. I must have known it was from you and put it on for our date."

"That makes my day."

She frowned.

"What?"

"Brady asked about it when I came out of the bedroom after I dressed."

"Why would he? Surely he's seen it. And he knows we're a couple." Jonathan hated that Langston had been at her place so much while he was in Chicago, but especially tonight when she was getting dressed to go out with *him*. The guy had purposely waited until Jonathan had gotten there and told him to get her home early.

"You and Brady don't get along, do you?" Clarissa asked.

"Did he say that?"

"No. But it's pretty obvious whenever I see you together, and every time you talk about each other."

"We're not much alike, Clarissa."

"I can tell that. But I care about you both. I know I do."

"Yes, honey, you do. But sometimes it hurts that you remember more about the three of them than about me."

"I'm sorry. Like I said, maybe now that you're back, it will be different."

"Maybe. I care about you so much."

The dinner was terrific, and he enjoyed hearing Clarissa analyze the food. Apparently Langston didn't like it when she was critical, saying she ruined the meal, but Jonathan enjoyed her comments. He enjoyed everything about her.

They ordered the chocolate bombe for dessert to share, and were halfway through the warm cake and creamy mousse filling when he reached over with his thumb to wipe some ice cream from the corner of her mouth. He left his hand there for a moment, his fingers underneath her chin. "You are so lovely, Clarissa. Sometimes you take my breath away."

A genuine, grateful smile. "Why, thank you." She blushed beautifully. "Let me return the favor by telling you how good you look in that sports coat."

"Thank you." He picked up her hand and kissed her fingers, just as a shadow fell over them. They both looked up.

"I thought that was you two cuddling over here in the corner."

Clarissa smiled ingenuously at the two women who'd come to the table. The striking, blue-eyed, dark-haired one had spoken. "I'm sorry, I'm afraid I don't remember you," Clarissa said.

"Lucky you."

"Excuse me?"

"I'm Brady's sister Samantha."

Clarissa looked pleased. "Oh, hi. Nice to meet you. Brady told me he came from a large family."

"No memories at all?" Samantha's tone was cool.

"They're coming back. Slowly, though."

The other woman spoke. "Hello, Clare."

Again, the blank looks. Maybe this would help Jonathan's cause. Maybe she'd recognize both these women, who were not a pleasant part of her life.

"Hello. I'm afraid I don't remember you, either."

"That's okay, we don't know each other well. I'm Lucinda Gray, Sam's friend from high school."

"Ah, how nice. Do you know Brady?"

The woman's laugh was off-kilter. "You might say that."

"Lucinda is Brady's girlfriend, Clare," Samantha inserted.

Clarissa stiffened. "Brady has a girlfriend?"

"I'm surprised he didn't tell you. He's been spending so much time with you."

"I…I'm sorry if…I didn't know." Clarissa's face drained of color and her hands covered her temples. "Oh, oh, God, my head."

"What is it?" Jonathan asked.

"A lot of pain." She looked faint, pale, sick.

Jonathan stood. "Excuse us, ladies. I'm taking Clarissa home."

At least both women seemed concerned. Samantha said, "Sorry if seeing us caused that."

After leaving his credit card with the waiter, Jonathan escorted Clarissa out, cursing the pain she was in. And as he got her to the car and she moaned, he tried to tell himself that seeing Samantha was what had caused the attack. Not finding out that Langston had a girlfriend.

"WHAT THE HELL DID YOU DO to her?" Brady asked when Jonathan practically dragged Clare down the corridor. He was waiting for them, standing in the doorway to his place, so he must have been watching as they pulled into the driveway.

"She's sick, and it's your fault," Jonathan said.

"No, of course it isn't." Clare's headache had abated on the drive there but her stomach felt queasy. All she wanted was to lie down.

She caught a glimpse of Brady's face, his expression worried.

"I'm all right now." She managed to walk through her own door without assistance.

Brady followed them in, but Clare went straight to her bedroom. She wasn't up to watching the two men she obviously cared about go another round. She undressed without putting her clothes away, slipped on pajamas, washed her face and brushed her teeth, then went back out into the bedroom. Glancing at the door, she shook her head and crawled into bed. But because their voices were raised, she could hear them outside her door.

"What exactly did Samantha say to her?" Brady's strong voice, angry now.

Equally strong came Jonathan's retort. "It's not what she said. It's what she implied. I don't know what you've been feeding your family about Clarissa, but it's obvious Samantha hates her."

"My sister does not hate her."

"Your girlfriend didn't help."

Clare strained to hear Brady's answer. "Lucy was there?" Lucy, not Lucinda.

"Yeah, and she was hostile to Clarissa."

"She's always been jealous of Clare," he said absently.

Really? Hmm. Clare wondered why.

"Oh, that's just great." A pause. "I'm tired of talking about this, Langston. You can leave now."

"Why would I leave?"

"Because you're not needed here. I'm back from my trip, and I'm staying over." A pause. "It won't be the first time, as you well know."

"Damn it, Harris, you're not going to put the moves on her now." Brady's voice had risen a notch. "She doesn't remember who the hell you are."

Oh, no! Clare hoped that wasn't Jonathan's intention. She shivered at the thought and burrowed further into the covers.

"That's none of your goddamned business."

"Clare's welfare is my business." Another pause, then a slam of the door.

After a few minutes, she heard Jonathan come to the bedroom. He didn't turn on the light, but eased his way inside. Clare knew she should talk to him, knew she shouldn't pretend she was asleep. But she had a lot to think about.

The exchange between Brady and Jonathan.

Why Brady's sister hated her.

And why, when Samantha introduced Lucinda as Brady's girlfriend, Clare's heart hurt worse than her head.

So she kept her eyes closed and feigned sleep until it came.

IN THE MIDST OF A GRAY FOG, Clare hid in the bushes. She was freezing cold, the branches dug into her skin and her hands were numb. People were searching for her. Terrified, she crowded back into the cover of the foliage and the fog where she could hear them but they wouldn't see her. One thing she was sure of: she had to avoid getting caught at all costs.

"Where is she?" Jonathan's voice was raised, angry.

"I have no idea. I'm worried." Brady's tone mirrored his words.

"I don't believe you, Langston. You're doing everything in your power to keep her from me."

"Ditto, Harris."

"I had her." Jonathan was yelling now. "I don't have to get her back."

"I know the reason she got in the accident. None of you can fool me any longer."

At Brady's words, Clare felt compelled to sneak out from behind the bushes. She could see both men, dressed in cowboy clothes, facing down each other. When he tipped his head back, she saw Brady's face was furious. A pink glow emanated from him.

Jonathan was in an orange haze. "Like hell you do."

"I do."

Suddenly, a crowd of little girls came rushing toward them, all dressed in Girl Scout uniforms. One was Catherine. Then Lucinda and two others she recognized as Brady's sisters.

Brady smiled, motioned them to come closer.

"They won't help," Jonathan said, nodding to the girls who stood behind Brady. "Nothing's going to help you now, Langston."

Growing in size, bigger, broader, Brady slid his hand to the gun holstered against his thigh. The girls behind him were screaming, crying, telling him to stop, that Clare wasn't worth it.

Abruptly, the scene switched. Clare was somewhere

else. In a room with no doors. It was pitch-black in here. She couldn't see anyone, just hear them moving around. From her hiding place, she whispered, "I'm sorry. God, Jonathan, I'm so, so sorry."

BRADY WENT WHERE HE ALWAYS went when he was upset. He drove through the deserted city streets out to the Rockford suburb where he'd grown up, pulled his car into the driveway of the big house and stared at the exterior. Still the same slate-gray siding, sheltering three floors that had been home to two parents, five kids and an assortment of dogs, cats and rabbits over the years. Wishing his dad were still alive, he sighed heavily. Mel Langston had been an ideal father, not that Brady hadn't butted heads with him. He was killed trying to save a kid from a burning building. Brady could still picture the firefighter funeral with all its gravity. He ached whenever he thought of it.

Swearing at himself for adding more problems to his night by reminiscing about his dad, he got out of his truck, climbed the steps to the front porch and went inside. It was ten at night, but his mother would be up. She had a nurse's penchant for late hours and early morns, as she still worked part-time at one of the local hospitals.

What he didn't expect was to find Samantha at the kitchen table with her. The two women looked alike with dark hair—his mother's graying some—and blue eyes. Brady and his two brothers had the same coloring, but their facial features resembled his dad.

"Hey," he said, trying not to show his anger at Sam for what she'd done in the restaurant. As the oldest, he was always protecting his sisters, even from himself.

Sam looked up. "I'm sorry."

He chuckled. "Well, that takes the wind out of my sails."

Crossing to the table where they sat drinking wine, he kissed Samantha's head, then his mother's. She clasped his hand and squeezed it briefly. "There's my boy."

He grabbed a beer from the fridge and joined them. He took a swig—the cold liquid felt good on his parched throat—and watched them.

Sammy finally said, "You can yell at me, Brady. I hate her, but I feel bad about upsetting her. I thought she was going to throw up all over Jonathan's thousand-dollar suit."

"We're not that lucky."

"Hush," his mom said, but her eyes held mirth.

Brady blew out a heavy breath. "Things are a mess."

"What else is new?" Sam asked. "Clare leaves disaster in her wake."

There was a blast of a horn outside. "Saved by the bell," his mom announced. To Brady she added, "That's Jimmy. He's come to pick Sam up, and Lizzy's in the car, so he's not coming in."

"Give him my best." Brady accepted his sister's hug warmly and held on just a bit longer. His anger diffused as quickly as it had come. "And hug my niece."

When Samantha left to join her husband and child, Brady's mother turned to him. "You can tell me. I won't criticize Clare."

"I know, you always liked her."

"Very much. She just lost her way, and I'm sorry you got hurt by it."

He knocked back more beer, not wanting to think about the past two years, not wanting to admit his guilt, his terror and his confusion.

"Sammy told me most of what happened tonight at the restaurant."

"I only got filled in by Harris." His fist curled around the bottle. "I hate that man."

"Honey…"

"I know it won't do any good." He looked after Sam. "She shouldn't have said anything to Clare, but I can't stand being mad at any of them."

"Which is why you left your job and your marriage in Chicago when your dad died and came back home."

"No, Mom. I came home because I was sick of being away from all of you. I never really wanted to stay there after art school. When I sold my first book, I could have moved back. But Gail wasn't having any of it."

"I still felt bad about your marriage breaking up over us."

"My marriage was over long before I left Gail. And the point isn't that I moved back then, it's that I should have moved back before Dad died."

"So you said."

"Doesn't matter. It's a done deal. And if I hadn't moved back to Rockford, I wouldn't have met Clare."

His mother's expression was grave. "Which in some ways would have been a good thing, given the circumstances."

He shook his head.

"How long has it been since the accident?"

"Seventeen days and twenty hours."

"Oh, honey. And she still doesn't remember you?"

"*Nada.*" He shrugged. "But she's getting flashes of our past together. Thankfully, it's early on, when things were pretty good between us."

"It'll all come back."

He averted his face. His mother had always been able

to read her children like books. He was the easiest. From bringing frogs into his bedroom, to cutting school, to the first time he had sex, there had been no secrets between them.

Except one. Now.

"You want that, don't you, Brade? For Clare to remember?"

Sadness filled him. It happened every time he thought about Clare's accident. And he was so tired of keeping this to himself. "Maybe not."

"What aren't you telling me?"

"Something I haven't told anyone."

When he didn't go further, couldn't, she took his hand. "I won't judge, I promise."

"I know you won't. It's just hard admitting this to you. I'm…ashamed of myself."

"Tell me, son."

"The reason Clare was out on the road late that night?"

His mother nodded.

"It was my fault, Mom. I caused Clare's accident and memory loss. And I'll never forgive myself."

CHAPTER SIX

"NOTHING LOOKS FAMILIAR?" Jonathan asked as he and Clare stood on the set of *Clarissa's Kitchen*.

It was easy to tell he was disappointed, Clare thought. Sometimes he looked so unhappy, it made her feel guilty for not remembering things. That, coupled with the anxiety still stirring inside her from the dream last night, had her wishing she hadn't come to the studio today.

"No, I'm sorry, nothing."

She studied the show's set—a nicely laid out space with a steel refrigerator to the audience's right, built-in ovens on the left and the counter cooktop facing the cameras. The walls were a creamy-yellow, and wooden cabinets graced the area. There was even a fake window with pretty wooden shutters. But in contrast to her own kitchen, Clare felt chilled by the strangeness of the place, even though she'd seen the set, at least an earlier version of it, on the tape she and Brady had watched.

Also disconcerting were the people who knew her when she walked into the studio this morning. She remembered no one. Several WRNY staffers greeted her, asked how she was and wished her well. She wondered if they liked her. God, she hoped she wasn't a prima donna.

Gently, Jonathan touched her arm. "Maybe we should try your dressing room."

"Whatever you think."

He led the way, with her next to him. As usual, he was dressed in a suit that was beautifully tailored. "Are your suits handmade?" she asked.

Stopping just as they entered a hallway off the set, he turned to her. "Yes. I brought you to my tailor. He makes all your clothes for the show."

"I…I saw them in my closet." Beautiful outfits in a variety of styles, none of which she recognized as her own. She hadn't worn any of them yet, and today was dressed in a casual one-piece sage-green outfit with short sleeves and cropped legs. A chunky necklace and a three-strand green faux pearl bracelet she'd found in the jewelry box matched the clothes perfectly. "I feel comfortable dressed like this for some reason."

Jonathan's face tightened. "For now, you don't need to wear anything more…chic. We do have to talk about the shooting schedule for the winter. It starts in July."

They were on hiatus, Clare had been told, but more shows needed to be taped before the end of the year. Still…

"Jonathan, you don't expect me…I can't…I don't remember anything. How can I possibly film a show?"

"Don't panic." He took her hand in his. It calmed her, as did the understanding in his gaze. Those kinds of looks, the soothing, heartfelt ones, made her more comfortable with him. "I won't push you to do anything. It's just that…"

"What?"

"You're being considered for other things. There's been talk of moving the show to the Cooking Channel."

"Really? That's good, isn't it?"

"Very. Do you remember the Cooking Channel?"

"Yes. Ramona Rich. The Barefoot Princess. I watched

some on TV this week and knew about the people and the programs."

His whole demeanor brightened. "I'm glad. That means you're getting back to your old life."

She frowned, thinking of what she'd learned about her *old life* in the past six days. "Brady said I have a cookbook in the works, too. It sounds like a lot for one person to do. I'm not sure I'm up to doing both now. Truthfully, I wonder how I ever did it all."

"You won't have to worry about that." He didn't meet her gaze. "The, um, cookbooks will be ancillary if the show is picked up nationally."

That didn't sound right. "It's a bit much to take in."

"Let's go sit and talk about this."

They headed down the long corridor and reached the dressing rooms. On her door was what she recognized as one of Brady's designs. He'd painted a big pink star with a blond, green-eyed female face on it. She chuckled.

"How adorable."

"That's our Brady." Jonathan took out a key and opened the room.

She stepped inside ahead of him. Very classy. Grass cloth walls, a vanity table with a large mirror surrounded by small lightbulbs. And a white leather couch across the way. It smelled like the fresh flowers that sat on the table.

She crossed to them. "These are lovely."

"Thanks. I thought they might cheer you up. You like roses."

Delia's words in the garden came back to her. *Your favorite flowers are carnations.* Often it felt like her friends from the condo and Jonathan were talking about two different people. Or that the amnesia had made her schizophrenic.

Shrugging, she crossed to the couch and sat. "Sit down, Jonathan. I want to discuss what happened last night."

When she'd awakened this morning, Jonathan had made coffee and was ready to go home and change. He'd spent the night on the couch. He'd made it clear he wasn't interested in conversation, so she let it go. But after the dream, especially, she wanted to talk to him.

He dropped down beside her. "What did Langston say about his sister?"

"I haven't seen him. I went next door after you left, but he wasn't there."

"Maybe he spent the night with Lucinda."

Her heart gave a little lurch. The thought of Brady with the beautiful woman was…unpleasant.

"When I went into my bedroom last night, I heard you arguing. What's going on between you two? I know I asked you before and you only said you were different kinds of people. But I sense a lot of hostility, and I want to know what the real problem is."

His face flushed, and she saw his hands curl into fists. Obviously, this was a sore subject, one that angered him. He looked at the ceiling. When he turned back to her, he seemed more in control. "When I came into your life, Clarissa, he and his buddies had to make room for me. They made it very clear that they didn't like sharing you."

"They said I got busy at work."

"Yes. And you and I became involved. We spent a lot of time at the station and together socially. I guess you could say I took you away from them." He shrugged a shoulder. "To be fair, I don't blame them for that. I'd feel the same if they snatched up all your time." His hand fisted again. "But I hate Langston's possessiveness about you."

For the life of her, she couldn't remember the dynamics of these relationships. Literature about amnesia said the memories closer to the trauma came back last, but this animosity between Brady and Jonathan had obviously been going on for years. Suddenly, the snake dream and the cowboy dream made sense to her. And frightened her. She'd been so vulnerable in both scenarios.

Gently, Jonathan picked up her hand. "Did you hear me, Clarissa? I said we were close. We spent our nights together, too."

Uh-oh.

"You don't remember making love with me, do you?"

A quick vision of tangled bodies and sweaty flesh flashed through her mind. There was a fleeting sensation of heat and a burst of passion, then it was gone.

"Did you recall something?"

"An image." She swallowed hard. "And a feeling."

He leaned in close and slid his arm around her. His other hand rested on her throat intimately. "A sexual one?"

Again, the muscular feel of a man's body next to her, on top of her. Then a blinding sense of connection. Oneness.

"Yes."

"That's us, Clarissa, together." He looked in her eyes. "I'm dying to kiss you."

Pure panic seized her. "No, Jonathan, I'm not ready for that."

"It's been so long."

"Three weeks."

He watched her for a minute, then drew back. "You're right. I'm sorry. I didn't mean to push you." He gave her a cute grin. "You're pretty irresistible, though. And we had a good sex life."

He was so sweet and understanding about her refusal—about everything, really. Except her relationship with Brady. "It's nice of you to take this so well. It can't be easy. You've done so much for me since the accident."

"I'd do anything for you, honey. Any time." He stood. "I thought maybe you'd like to say hello to the show's producer now. I know he's in today, and he's been worried about you."

Clare was tired and wanted to go home. But as she'd said, Jonathan had done so much for her and despite what he'd said, it had to be difficult for him that she couldn't remember their intimacy. "That would be fine."

He drew her up by the hand and pulled her close. She cuddled in, trying harder to recall the feel of his chest, his scent—which was great—his physical presence. She didn't, but she felt more comfortable with him, at least. Maybe he was right. Now that he was back, maybe she'd remember being close to him.

He kissed the top of her head, and as they parted, something caught her eye. On the table next to the couch was a framed photo. She stooped over and picked it up. It was of her and Jonathan, on a beach. They were both dressed in swimsuits and smiling at the camera. They looked happy to be together. Once again, she wondered why she couldn't remember the joy of being with him, reflected so clearly in the picture.

BRADY WAS IN THE ATTIC, sweating off the effects of a fitful sleep. He hadn't come home last night, mostly because he couldn't bear the thought of being in the condo next to Clare's while she slept beside Harris.

And maybe did more.

So he'd bunked in his old room at his mother's house and tossed and turned all night long, thinking about Clare with Jonathan. Brady had gotten up about dawn and cooked his mother breakfast when she awoke. He'd come home to a note—at least Clare had done that—which said she'd gone to the station with Harris. Was she getting back to her old life so soon? The thought filled him with a familiar sadness and reminded him of times he wasn't sure he could go through again. So he'd headed up here to use the weights.

As he sat on a padded bench, he didn't start the reps right away. Instead, he took in the remodeled attic space. When they both started earning good money, he and Clare had hired a contractor to redo this area. They'd knocked down the walls between the attic over her condo and his, reinforced the floor and put in several skylights. Air-conditioning kept it cool in the summer and baseboard heating warmed it in the winter. Near the new windows was a Jacuzzi big enough for four. The rest was a large workout area and a bathroom. He'd picked free weights and a treadmill. Clare had added an elliptical to use when it was too cold to run outside. They both agreed on a TV, which over the years had been upgraded to a 52-inch entertainment center. He could watch sports from anywhere in the attic, and she could catch a show on the Cooking Channel. The room was a real perk, and they'd been lucky to have the space included in their purchase price.

What'll we do when one of us moves out? he'd asked Clare.

Whoever moves out first, the other gets ownership.

They'd even put it in writing.

And before the accident, Brady had been very close to

owning the whole attic floor of the old Victorian. He let the memory come, exacerbated by his presence in the attic, in *their* space, where they'd also come to be alone, talk or figure out a problem. When the images of what had gone on up here became too much for him to think about without going crazy, Brady picked up the remote and turned the TV on to a sports channel. As he watched the highlights of a Yankees game, he did arm curls and leg lifts until his muscles burned and he was breathing hard.

Just as he stopped, he heard behind him, "Wow!"

Clare came into his line of vision. She was wearing one of his favorite outfits. And a necklace he'd bought her.

"Hey, there. You must be feeling better."

"I am." She smiled weakly. "I heard the TV from the hallway downstairs because you left the door open." Once again she scanned the area. "What *is* all this?"

His heart clutched in his chest at her not remembering their pet project together—or, more importantly, the time they'd spent up here. "Joint property." He gave her the skinny on what they'd done.

"It's so cool." She crossed to the Jacuzzi. "I love this, don't I?"

"You know you do?"

"Uh-huh." She sat on the edge of the padded tub. Her hair was soft and wavy around her face and she pushed back the locks that fell over her eyes. "Like I said, I just know some things."

He gave her a weak smile.

She watched him as he picked up a towel and wiped the sweat off his face. "Brady, we need to talk about last night, but you can finish your workout first."

"No, now's fine. I need a break."

"Your sister doesn't like me. I could tell at the restaurant. Is it because of the too-busy-at-work stuff?"

Partly. "I think so."

"And you have a girlfriend." She clasped the necklace in her palm like a talisman. "Right?"

"Lucy and I date. It's not serious."

Her delicate sandy brows knitted. "It is to her."

He stretched out his legs to ease his tight muscles. "What makes you think that?"

"Women's intuition."

"I've been honest with her about how I feel, Clare." Well, not totally, not since the accident, but he couldn't tell Clare that. "She wants more from the relationship than I do, but she agreed to my terms."

"And you don't want more with her."

"I haven't in the past."

Clare stared at him.

"What?" he asked.

"Something about this is familiar. Did we do this often? Talk about personal things?" She scanned the area. "Here?"

"We were best friends. We came up here a lot and confided in each other." *Don't ask,* Brady warned himself. *Don't ask.* "Speaking of which, did Harris stay with you last night?" He hated himself for interrogating her, but he had to know.

"He slept on the couch." Her gaze narrowed on him. "Do you really think I'd— Hell, is that how you see me? That I'd have sex with somebody I didn't remember?"

"I thought maybe last night with him might bring your memory back."

"Nothing like that happened!" She still seemed offended. And irked. There was an edge in her voice when she asked, "What about you? Where'd you go last night?"

"To my mother's."

"Oh." She arched her brows. "Oh! Brady, I know her. She's tall, sturdily built, pretty hair the color of yours, but with some gray in it." A big smile. "She likes me."

He chuckled, recalling his mother and Clare cooking. How his mom had come over and tended to her when she got the flu. Clare taking her shopping.

"She does like you. I stayed out at her place because it was late and she likes it when I'm there." Which was true but not the truth.

Now her eyes darkened. "Oh, your dad. He's dead."

"A fire." He told her about the untimely death of the man he'd adored.

She got up from the tub, came toward him, and sat on the bench. Taking his hand in hers, she smiled sadly. "I wish I could remember him."

"That's not the amnesia, sweetheart. He was dead before I met you. It's why I came back to Rockford. I stayed with my mother for a while, then when this place came open in Max's building—we were friends in high school—I jumped at the chance to buy it."

"Still, I'm sorry for your loss."

God, could this get any harder? "You helped me, Clare, more than the others. I missed him so much, and telling you about him, commiserating with you about your parents and your grandmother, made us bond quickly."

"I'm so glad, Brady." She thought a moment. "Obviously, I know nothing about your life before you came back. If I never remember, will you tell me sometime?"

"Yeah, sure."

Clare stood. "Well, I'll let you get back to working out. I'm going downstairs."

"I don't have much longer." She started away but he snagged her hand. It felt soft and feminine in his, but he knew there was strength in it, too. "You okay?"

"Sure."

"You're not. You're sad."

"I guess I am. It's so hard not remembering things like your family or how close I was to you or Jonathan. And I'm having terrible dreams." She frowned. "I get scared a lot. It's hell being an adult and being frightened by what's out there in the world."

"I'm sorry. I have an idea for today, though, to cheer you up. And give you some bearings. Remember I told you we were working on a book?" She nodded. "Want to go look at it?"

"Oh, Brady, I'd love to. It'll make me feel better, won't it?"

"Uh-huh. Cooking, the books, always did." He pointed to the bathroom. "I'll clean up after I finish and come down."

She glanced at her watch. "I'll make us some lunch."

"That'll be great."

After she left, he did some stretches, then headed for the shower. His mood had changed, too. Working on their books also made him feel better. For now, he'd content himself with that.

IN HER KITCHEN, CLARE WENT to her cookbooks and plucked out one that had breakfast and lunch recipes. Scanning the table of contents, her gaze stopped at frittata.

Sausage, peppers, onions, potatoes. She remembered the recipe without looking at it. Flipping to the designated page, she saw she was right. There was an anecdote with this one.

One of my favorite memories is of my Grandma making frittata for Grandpa.

Suddenly, she saw the older man, big, balding and boisterous, grab her grandma around the waist while she cooked at the stove.

Cosmo Boneli had his favorites, and Grandma adored cooking for him. Her world revolved around him, and I can still see them walking together, holding hands, with the Tuscan countryside as a backdrop. Cathy and I would scamper in front of them, and he'd sneak a kiss when he thought we weren't watching.

Tears welled in Clare's eyes. She'd loved them both so much and felt their loss as if it had just happened. The same thing occurred when she had the flashback of Don Kramer. She remembered them moving to America to take care of her and Cathy, Grandpa's funeral then Grandma's death as if it was yesterday. When the blur cleared, she looked at the other page. Good Lord! There were her grandparents, walking hand in hand, little girls in front of them. This was Brady's drawing. He'd done it from pictures, she now remembered. Lovingly she traced her grandma's face. Her grandpa's big shoulders. Cathy's dainty dress. The drawing was so beautiful she didn't want to look away and stared at it for a long time.

Finally forcing herself to go to the freezer, she found sausage stored there along with separate packages of peppers and onions. She got eggs out of the fridge, spices from the cupboard and potatoes from the pantry. After she defrosted everything, she put the meat into a frying pan and the phone rang.

Clare didn't like talking on the phone these days. She answered Jonathan's calls on her cell, but mostly she let the machine pick up here. It was like the e-mails on her computer, which she didn't know how to answer. All the unfamiliar voices and the e-mails from people she obviously knew but didn't remember made her panic. She listened to the phone messages later, and Brady helped her wade through her e-mail so her in-box wouldn't get overloaded.

When the machine clicked on, she heard, "Clare, hi."

I miss Mommy and Daddy.

I do, too. But you have me, Cath, you always will. And Grandma and Grandpa.

Because she recognized this voice, she snatched up the receiver. "Cathy, is that you?"

"Clare! Does this mean you got your memory back?"

"No, I recognized your voice."

Sniffles on the other end. Her sister was crying.

"Oh, Cath. I'm starting to remember things. Your voice brought back a flashback of when we were little. And I've had others of you, too."

"When you were in the hospital, you said you didn't remember me at all."

"I—it's coming back." Not quite a lie. "A lot about when we were kids." She'd also gone through some of the photo albums and seen pictures of her slim, blond sister throughout their lives. But there weren't many from the past few years. "I remember what you look like."

"I'm so sorry I'm not there."

"You're in France, honey." Clare fell into the affectionate term easily. "Enjoy yourself."

"Hah! I took my students here to study the culture, but they're finding a million ways to get into trouble."

"I want to hear all about the trip. And everything else you do."

"I'll come to Rockford as soon as I get back."

"I can't wait to see you."

"Truly?"

No, not again. Clare had alienated so many people in her life. "Yes, truly. We can get in our pajamas at four o'clock and watch romantic comedies on Lifetime TV. Oh! I remember that, too."

"I'm so glad. Now tell me how you're feeling. About your progress."

She talked to her sister as she prepared the frittata. She used to do that a lot, cook and talk. By the time she hung up she was more optimistic about her recovery. She finished with the toast just as Brady came into the room, looking big and beautiful in denim shorts and a white T-shirt tucked in at the waist. It showed off all those muscles he'd been using upstairs.

He sniffed. "Frittata?"

"Yes. I had the ingredients frozen."

"Did you remember it was a favorite of mine?"

Why wasn't she surprised? "I think I might have, Brady. And Grandpa's, too." She held up the cookbook. "The drawing is beautiful. It spurred real, concrete memories of them."

"Super."

"Go sit, and we'll eat. I want to tell you about Cathy's phone call."

Brady took a seat at the table, and when Clare brought the plates, she set hers down first, then his. As she leaned over him, she was hit with the scent of him after a shower. It was so potent, so *familiar,* that it took her breath away. Shakily she put the plate in front of him.

"Something wrong?" he asked. "You're flushed."

Her hands went to her cheeks. "Must be the heat from the stove."

But she'd lied. It wasn't that. It was heat…but from Brady himself.

Because, when Clare got close to him and caught his scent, she felt her body tighten, her pulse speed up and a low coil of reaction in her belly.

All signs that were familiar.

All signs she remembered.

How could this be? She didn't understand. Why in hell was she *aroused* by Brady's nearness, the male smell of him, the physical presence of him? *Brady,* her best friend?

CHAPTER SEVEN

"THESE ARE THE RECIPES and the illustrations we've done for the seventh book."

They were in Brady's office, where they always worked, Clare in her favorite chair, and Brady across from her, perched on the edge of his desk. He watched her on the leather lounger as she flipped through the twenty or so pages he'd printed out. She looked rested and comfortable in jeans and a T-shirt that said Feed the Stomach, Feed the Soul. She wasn't flushed anymore, and he was still wondering what had caused the reaction when she'd served him the meal. She said she hadn't gotten a memory flash.

She glanced up from the work. "How many recipes do we need per cookbook?"

"We're halfway there."

Her brows arched. "People buy a cookbook for only forty recipes?"

"They buy your cookbook for the anecdotes and my illustrations, too, I like to think."

She cocked her head. "Brady, how am I supposed to come up with anecdotes if I don't remember anything from my past?"

"We've got ten more recipes and stories in draft form on your computer. We can start with those." He smiled.

"Maybe by the time we're finished polishing them, you'll have your memory back, babe."

"I'm worried about the anecdotes. I've tried reading some in the newer cookbooks, and contrary to the memory I just had about the frittata, they bring on headaches."

"You could always use some recipes from your other books." He shifted in his seat. "We did that in the last few because you were too busy to come up with more." And they had had a huge fight about what had been Harris's suggestion.

Frowning, she shook her head. "That sounds like cheating the reader. No, we'll think of something else."

"Ready?"

"I hope so."

"We'll take it slow. If it starts to make you uncomfortable or brings on a headache, we'll stop."

"Should I get my laptop?"

"No, we have shared files. I can call up your work here." Because he'd done a lot of the work without her, but he didn't tell her that.

"Clever."

He sat down at the computer and was booting up her recipes when the office phone rang. "I'll let it ring. It's probably one of my sisters. When I don't answer my cell, they call here, even though they know I'm working." He smiled affectionately at the phone. "Some things never change. When we were growing up, they'd barge into my room whenever they pleased." He shook his head. "They'd flop on my bed to talk, or borrow my shirts or snoop in my drawers."

"It sounds like you love them very much." She swallowed hard. "I wish Samantha didn't dislike me."

"She'll come around."

The answering machine clicked on, and it wasn't one of the girls. Leo's voice sounded from the machine. "Brady, if you're there, pick up."

"Who's that?" Clare asked.

"My agent."

Clare had been told she had her own agent, too, though she was currently on maternity leave and out of touch. Clare had gotten flowers from her publisher and spoken to her editor briefly on the phone.

"Okay, you're not there. Listen, Random House called. They're interested in the new series we discussed. They want to see a proposal. My guess is they're willing to offer big bucks. I know you're worried about Clare, but you can't do what you did before, buddy. You've got to keep *your* career on track. Call me with a date for the contract ASAP. Hope you're all right."

When he clicked off, the room was completely silent. Clare stared over at Brady from the chair, where she looked small and fragile again. "Well," she said, "this isn't good."

"It isn't as bad as it sounds."

"What exactly did you do last time? And don't lie to me."

"I'd never lie to you." *Keep things from you, yes, but never lie.* Though even not telling her everything was battering at his conscience.

"So what was your agent talking about?"

"When the cookbook thing took off, I put my own work aside." Which was a huge understatement, as well as a huge mistake.

"Why?"

"Because the cookbooks were important to you and to me. I needed a change of pace, anyway. I often do, which is why the idea of the new series my agent mentioned came up."

"How many books do you have out?"

"Ten, besides the cookbooks. I published three before I came back to Rockford."

She looked around the office. "Where are they?"

"On the shelves behind you."

Standing, Clare crossed to the bookcase and stared at the children's books he'd done. She took out five, set them on the floor, then took out the other five. Then she dropped down next to them, leaned against the bottom shelves and picked up one Brady recognized as his first book.

"What are you doing?"

"I'm going to read these."

"We have work to do."

She glanced at the phone. "Apparently, so do you. Alone. Go ahead and do something for your own stuff. I'll read."

"All of them?"

"Yes, every single one. Now hush."

For a minute, Brady could barely contain what he was feeling. He remembered the Clare of the past, reading his work, encouraging him, celebrating his successes. For a while she had been more excited than he was about each new book. Then things had changed. He wasn't sure she'd even read the last one, which had cut him to the core.

As he watched her open the first book, he swallowed hard. She read the dedication—to his dad—and the bio information. Then she started the story of Millie and Raoul. At one point, she traced the illustrations of the shy mouse and the grumpy rat with her finger. She chuckled at the antics of the rodents. Grinned hugely. After she finished the first book, she looked up. He'd been staring at her the whole time, observing the play of emotions over her face. "I'm in awe. These had to be a big hit."

"They were."

Still smiling, she went on to the second. Feeling foolish because he was staring at her, he tried to work, but he kept being distracted by her laughter, her exclamations, her sniffles. "Oh, no, Millie lost her mama."

"Yeah, kids across America learned about death."

She shook her head, sending wisps of hair into her eyes. "Incredible."

He needed to stop staring at her, so he got up and crossed to his drafting table, thinking he could start some sketches for the new book. Then she startled him. "Oh, Brady."

Right away he knew why she held up book five. Nostalgia drifted through him like a warm Caribbean breeze. "I'd moved in here by then," he said, his voice husky. "And we got close."

In that particular book, it was the dedication that had made her eyes go misty. "That's quite an honor. Thank you so much."

Brady remembered it word for word.

To my dearest Clare, who means more to me than I can express. Thank you for your friendship, your support and your loyalty.

"Was I excited?"

"Thrilled." She'd hugged him as if she'd never let him go. He missed those spontaneous, uncensored hugs.

By the time she finished reading all ten of his stories, it was late afternoon and he'd gotten little work done. She smoothed the cover of the last one lovingly and set it on the stack. Her expression was sad. "I'm so sorry you put this aside for me."

"For us."

"Whatever. I'll bet kids are clamoring for more."

"So the publisher says. I've got one to finish now. The last of Millie and Raoul."

Standing, she replaced the books and faced him. "I'm going to go back to my condo so you can work on their story."

"No, don't go. My creative energy is drained. Besides, Max and Delia and I are having movie night at Max's on his big-screen TV, and I'm responsible for the food."

She glanced at the clock.

"I'd ask you to come, but I heard you talking to Harris about going out with him tonight."

Her shoulders sagged. "I'm supposed to. Maybe if I took a nap, I'd have more energy for that."

"Sounds like a plan."

Glancing away, she noticed a photo on the shelf and picked it up. It was of Max, Delia, Brady, Clare and Don Kramer, all a lot younger, barbecuing out back. Brady's hair was longer, Clare's was curly and Max hadn't shaved his head yet. The most striking thing about it, Brady knew, was how happy Dee and Don were.

Clare stared at the photo for a long time, then shook her head. "Could I use your phone a second?"

"Sure." From the drafting table, he watched her curiously as she crossed to his desk.

"Do you have Jonathan's cell number?"

What was she up to? "Um, yeah. He gave it to me after you got hurt."

He joined her at the desk and fished the number out of his Rolodex. She punched it in. And waited, without looking at him.

"Hello, Jonathan?" She paused. "Yes, I'm feeling well.

But I'm going to cancel our dinner plans. No, no. I'd like to stay in tonight. Regroup a bit." A longer pause. "Please, I don't want you to do that. Yes, I'll call you tomorrow."

She set the receiver in its cradle and peered up at Brady with an expression he couldn't read. "I didn't lie," she said.

"I heard. Fudged the truth a bit."

She cocked her head. "I…I'd rather be with you guys tonight."

"Music to my ears, babe."

"Will it be all right with Max and Delia?"

"I'm sure it will."

"Okay. I think I'll go nap now." Her face brightened. "And I'll make some dessert. What do you guys like?"

"Your brownies are Max's favorite. The ones with the butterscotch bits in them."

She nodded to the computer. "You work on those wonderful stories." Leaning over, she kissed his cheek, something she used to do routinely but hadn't for a while.

Her scent—the lotion and shampoo—made Brady's gut clench. He wanted to hold her so badly, he ached. He had to stifle the images that played through his mind.

She drew back and walked out of the office. Suddenly he was energized. And happy. And hopeful.

For the first time in over a year, Clare had chosen Brady over Jonathan.

IT WAS SO PLEASANT, BEING IN the warm water, letting the jets swirl around her. Clare felt safe, secure, loved. Opening her eyes, she looked out the attic window and saw snow had begun to fall—little flakes clung to the glass—making the heat rising from the tub even more delicious.

The door to the attic opened, and Brady stepped inside. He was naked and beautifully formed—a chest covered with dark hair, toned abs, muscular thighs. An impressive erection. She smiled.

"Don't gawk," he said teasingly. "You've seen it all before."

"Ah, but it's such a pleasant sight."

He held up the bottle he carried. "Champagne."

"What's the occasion?"

"You're back." Easily, he popped the cork. "Finally, you're back."

"I am." She sat up, revealing bare breasts. She knew she should be embarrassed in front of her best friend, but she wasn't.

As he came closer with two filled flutes, his gaze caressed her. Handing her a glass, he leaned over and kissed the swell of one breast, then climbed into the tub.

The water sloshed with his weight, and Brady held up his drink. "To new beginnings," he said easily.

"To new beginnings."

Lazing back in the tub, she closed her eyes again. Nothing was better than this, she thought, absolutely nothing.

Then the water turned freezing cold and she began to shiver. Oh, God, what was happening?

This time when she opened her eyes and looked over, the other man in the tub wasn't Brady. He was Jonathan. "What's going on?" she asked.

"What do you mean? Is something wrong?"

"Where's Brady?"

"Darling, Brady's gone. He's been gone a long time. I'm here now."

"I…"

"Shh," he said, taking the flute from her hand. "Relax. Lie back and enjoy the water."

"But it's cold."

"No, no, it isn't."

"I want Brady." She started to cry.

Suddenly Jonathan's face flushed with anger. "Don't you dare cry over another man in front of me."

"I'm sorry. I can't help it."

"Then get out…"

CLARE AWOKE. SHE WAS in her own bed, and she was warm. Outside, she could see the forsythia tree blooming by her window—no snow—and the sun was still shining. She glanced at the clock. 5:00 p.m. She had just enough time to make the brownies. Throwing off the light cover, she realized she was naked. And then she remembered the dream. Her head began to pound.

She made her way to the bathroom, took some Tylenol and dressed quickly. In the kitchen, she found the brownie recipe Max liked in volume two and began making the chocolate confection. She kept her mind busy because she didn't want to think about the dream. But after the pan was in the oven, she pulled out the notebook and, according to Anna's instructions, began recording the events.

She blushed writing about Brady's nakedness. Felt fear resurrect at Jonathan's anger. She tried to console herself with Anna's assurances.

Clare, dreams don't mean you necessarily want what you dream. They often combine reality in shocking ways.

She started to giggle. Well, being naked with her best friend was shocking, all right.

But she stopped giggling when she admitted that the

dream wasn't the only time she felt turned on by Brady. The sensations she'd experienced when serving him lunch today—becoming aroused, wanting more from him—confused her. And when she'd read his books, she'd been filled with warm feelings, which had gotten even warmer when she'd caught him watching her. What did all this mean?

It was nearing six when she took the brownies out of the oven and put the pan in a wicker nest she found in the cupboard. She stuck her keys in her pocket, crossed to the foyer and maneuvered open the door. It slammed behind her. At the sound, the woman in the hall startled. Lucinda Gray had her hand on the doorbell of Brady's condo.

She didn't have a key.

Clare remembered Brady's words. *She wants more, but she understands the terms.*

Lucinda faced Clare and shook back her thick auburn hair, and her heavily made-up hazel eyes widened. "Hello, Clare."

"Lucinda."

The other woman wore nice tan jeans with a sexy peach camisole that revealed a small unicorn tattoo on her shoulder. "You don't happen to know where Brady is, do you? I've rung four times."

"Um, no." The untruth came easily to her lips. Well, maybe it was only fudging again. She didn't know for *certain* if Brady was at Max's yet. He said he had to go out to pick up food.

Oh, hell, if she was honest with herself, she might as well admit that she didn't want Lucinda to horn in on the evening and was making a conscious decision to cut her out of the night.

"I thought you might know his schedule. These days he's always with you. I was just about to try your door."

"You alluded to that the other night, Lucinda. I know Brady's been with me a lot, and I'm sorry if that's affected your relationship." Another lie.

"I didn't say it affected us at all." She arched a pretty brow. "Brady and I are very close."

Apparently not enough to have a key to his place, one of which resided right now in Clare's pocket next to her own.

"I know you're close. He's a wonderful man, and I'm sure you appreciate him."

"Too bad you don't."

Clare bristled. But she decided she wasn't having this conversation with Brady's girlfriend. "If you'll excuse me…"

Lucinda nodded to the brownies. "Bringing food to a friend?"

"I am, yes."

"Have a good time."

"You, too, when you find Brady." Which Clare knew very well Lucinda wasn't going to do. "I'll walk out with you."

She descended the stairs, showed Lucinda the door and even walked outside with her and waited for the woman to leave. When she reentered the house, Clare was embarrassed by her actions. And she was also concerned, enough to have her pulse going double-time.

Why on earth would she deliberately lie to Brady's girlfriend?

CHAPTER EIGHT

"HI." CLARE SMILED AT MAX when he opened the door to his condo. The red golf shirt and khaki shorts looked good on him, making her wonder if there was a woman in his life. She was ashamed she hadn't asked since she'd come home from the hospital.

"Clare. I...wasn't expecting you."

Damn it. First she had that dream, then she lied to Lucinda, and now she barged in where she wasn't wanted. The last made her feel the worst. "Brady said to be here at six. I assumed that he told you I was coming." She held up the pan of brownies like a little girl offering a bribe. "I brought your favorite dessert."

"Brady didn't tell me." When she didn't say more, he added, "But it's cool. Come on in."

"Is Delia here yet?" she asked before stepping inside.

"No, it's her turn to pick the movies, so I imagine that's where she is."

Anxious because she could feel Max's hesitation, Clare crossed the threshold of his home. While he took the brownies and brought them to the kitchen, she studied the place. It was amazing how unique the four condos in the house were. Max's was painted in bold colors: deep-green for the living area, red in the dining room. Unlike hers, the latter was closed off by a wall; she could see through the doorway that there were no walls between it and the kitchen. Big stuffed couches in contrasting solid green and green-and-white stripes faced an oak entertainment center. Off to the left, where the office was in her own condo, the walls had been removed, and an open space sprawled out with a desk and more seating. "Your place is beautiful, Max," she told him when he returned.

"You helped me redecorate."

"I did? I wish I remembered that. Looks like I have good taste."

"Uh-huh." They were just inside the entryway. "Tell me why you're here."

Facing her friend, she stood tall and lifted her chin. "I guess I invited myself. Brady said you were having movie night, and I wanted to come."

Dark brows furrowed. "No plans with Harris?"

"You don't like him, either?"

"He's not my favorite person."

"I don't know what to say. I can leave, if I'll spoil your evening." Her voice caught on the last word. "As I said, I invited myself."

His expression softened immediately. "No, no. Look, let's sit. I don't want to upset you. We had a nice dinner at your home the other night. Let me be as hospitable."

"Thanks, Max."

They'd moved farther into the living room when the front door burst open and Delia rushed in, followed by Brady. She carried a paper bag. Brady toted a pizza box and, Clare deduced from the scent, probably hot wings in foam cartons.

"Hey, guys." Brady set the food down on Max's slate-topped coffee table, then his gaze zeroed in on Clare. "I'm glad you made it." She was disconcerted by the dream—seeing Brady *naked* in the dream—until he crossed to her and kissed her cheek. Suddenly everything seemed all right.

"Max didn't know I was coming."

Leaving a hand on her arm, Brady frowned. "It's okay, though, isn't it?" he asked his friend.

"Fine by me."

Clare looked to Delia and was shocked to see the woman was scowling. "Delia, don't you want me here?"

Cradling the bag to her chest, she shook her head. "It's not that. I… I'm afraid…" She looked to Brady. He seemed puzzled, too, until she handed him the bag and he drew out the contents. Videos.

When he saw what they were, he said to Delia, "It'll be all right, Dee," and to Clare, "They're movies about amnesia."

"I didn't know you'd be here," Delia rushed on to say. "I ordered these on the Internet last week. I wanted to see them to get insight…never mind, I'll go to the video store for something else."

Clare cocked her head. "I'm game. What did you get?"

"Hitchcock's *Spellbound* and *Anastasia, Memento, Dead Again* and *Regarding Henry*." The last was one Anna, Clare's therapist, had mentioned.

"At least I won't remember any I've seen."

Her levity broke the tension, and even Max gave a chuckle.

"We went to a Hitchcock festival at the Little Theater," Brady told her as they moved to sit. "You saw *Anastasia,* but I don't know if you've seen the others. *Dead Again* is great. Lucy and I watched it on video."

Clare didn't want to think about Lucinda Gray and her beautiful hair, big eyes and killer body. But she felt guilty about what she *hadn't* told the woman. So Clare straightened her shoulders and faced Brady. "I saw Lucinda in the hall in front of your condo, looking for you."

"Yeah? We don't have plans for tonight."

"Maybe you wanted her here. I should have said something."

"No outsiders on movie night," Max declared.

Feeling inordinately pleased by the fact that Lucinda was an outsider and she herself wasn't, Clare grinned. "Oh, okay then."

She and Brady took seats; Delia went into the kitchen and Max stood by the screen, his arms folded over his chest. "You knew you sat there, Clare?"

"I guess." She'd dropped down on the smaller couch with Brady. His jean-clad thigh rested against hers, and as always, his nearness settled her. Yet today, it was combined with an awareness, a tug of something else. "Do we always sit in the same places?"

"We used to," Max said. "I'm just surprised you know that when you don't remember anything else."

"Amnesia's odd like that." Brady opened the boxes. "Dig in."

Delia returned with four bottles of Corona. Clare had a quick vision of clinking identical bottles of beer with the people in the room. When she just stared at the one Delia held out to her, her friend asked, "Don't you drink this anymore?"

"I have no idea what I drink." She took the bottle and sipped. "Hmm, I like it."

The smell of the pizza was heavenly. Its sauce and cheesy scent caused another flash. "I have a pizza recipe in one of my books, don't I?" she asked Brady.

After chewing a mouthful, he nodded. "Uh-huh. Your aunt Patricia's. You've got ways to dress it up, too."

"Is there an anecdote about her in there?"

"Yes. From when you stayed with her and she let you and your cousins Kristen and Ryan play with dough."

Delia laughed. "It's one of Donny's favorites."

"Speaking of our half-pint," Max said affectionately, "when's he coming home, girl?"

"I go get him in eight days, four hours and—" she glanced at her watch "—thirty minutes. But who's counting?" Her grin was self-effacing. "I'm staying with Don's parents for a few days, then going to visit my mother, too."

"You must miss him," Clare remarked.

"I do." A pause. "He loves you, Clare. You helped raise him. I couldn't have done it without you after Don died."

Warmth flowed through Clare, like no other she'd felt. "He does? I'm so glad."

"Hey, what about us?" Brady asked.

"You guys helped, too. But you both *remember* that."

Max picked up the movies. "Which one first?"

"*Spellbound,*" Brady and Delia said together.

The haunting Hitchcock video began. Eerie strains of music echoed from the speakers, but they weren't familiar to Clare. She did realize how young Gregory Peck and Ingrid Bergman were, though.

"There's your lady, Langston," Max said when Bergman came on-screen.

Clare caught Max's tone. "What does that mean?"

"Brady has a thing for Ingrid."

Ingrid was in the first scene as a therapist with a patient. Clare's hands went to her face. "I look a little like her." She could feel her face flush. "Oh, not that you have a thing... Oh, geez..."

Brady chuckled. "You teased me about it before, sweetheart. I took to calling you Ingrid."

She had a quick flash of Brady yelling from the doorway, *Come on, Ingrid, we're going to be late for dinner.*

Mesmerized, Clare watched each scene unfold.

When John Ballantine, the main character and also a doctor, got his first headache and became faint because he remembered something, Clare pressed a hand against her stomach and took in a heavy breath. "I know just how he feels."

"You okay?" Brady asked, sliding an arm around her.

"I am." *Now,* she thought but didn't say, just leaned into him.

When, after only one day together, Constance and John declared their love, Max made a disgusted sound. "I hate these love-at-first-sight stories."

"That's how Don and I fell in love."

Picking up the remote, Max stopped the video. "Dee, I'm sorry. I forgot."

"It's okay. I know it's rare. But that's how it happened for us. Besides, I can think about the good things with Don without feeling bad."

"I'd like to hear about him and how you met, sometime," Clare told her.

Delia gave her a half smile. "We met at a frat party in college. You were there."

"We went to the University of Rockford, right?"

"Uh-huh. Don and I stayed here, and you went on to culinary school in Boston." She glanced at the guys, who were rolling their eyes at the girl talk. "I'll tell you more later."

The movie resumed and John's episodes continued. When he and Constance began talking about his amnesia,

Clare was surprised. For a film made in 1945, its medical insights into the syndrome were surprisingly current. The basic psychological premise: people developed amnesia to cover up a difficult event—the mind protects the body that way. The common physical cause: injury to the head. Clare rubbed her skull on the spot where she'd hit it in the car. Briefly, she closed her eyes because suddenly she could feel the pain.

His expression concerned, Max paused the movie again. "Clare, you okay?"

"Yes, I just keep wondering if the cause of my amnesia is psychological or physical."

For some reason, Brady stiffened.

Max told her, "The accident was at 2:00 a.m. Something had to have happened before it, to drive you out into the rainy night."

Delia leaned forward. "Honey, we already told you that Brady saw you earlier in the evening, here at home. But we don't know why you left or where you were headed."

Blurry images—like silhouettes—flashed through her mind. *Two people, a man and a woman, arguing.* When her head began to pound, she closed her eyes tightly this time.

"Maybe we should turn off the movie," Brady said.

"No." Clare shook herself. "I don't want to do that."

Later in the film, Constance told her colleague she was safe with John, that a person won't do anything with amnesia that he wouldn't normally do, Clare *did* quip, "That's what Anna Summers said. I'd hate to think I'd murder someone in his sleep."

Brady squeezed her hand. "You know, that also means good things. All the kindness and love you show now is innately you, too."

"Anna mentioned that."

The movie progressed to the point where John and Constance traveled to Rochester to see her old analyst and friend. Brady moved to the edge of the seat and absently put his hand on Clare's knee. "This is my favorite part."

The dream sequence in the movie gave Clare goose bumps. She'd kept the dream of her and Brady at bay since she'd come down to Max's, but it was there, in the back of her mind, complete with the warmth she'd felt with Brady and how everything had turned cold with Jonathan.

On the screen were peaked roofs, shadowy figures and a narration by John as he described the dream to the two therapists. The images were warped and elongated, and Clare wondered why Brady liked the scene so much. It came to her after the sequence was finished. "The sets were done by Salvador Dalí. I remember now. He's one of your favorite artists. We went to a show of his in New York."

Brady squeezed her knee. "Right, sweetheart."

"Did we go there often?"

"Yeah, the five of us. Sometime I'll tell you about Charlie's place, where we stayed."

Clare was riveted at the end of the film when all the secrets came out. Would hers? In a blinding flash like John's? And would she end up happily ever after, as he did?

They took a break before the next movie. The guys left to hit the head and Delia reached over and grabbed Clare's hand. "Did seeing the film help or hurt?"

"Actually, it helped. It confirmed a lot of what I feel. Especially the dreams and headaches stuff. Seeing the symptoms played out is different from being *told* what's happening to me."

"Still getting them?"

"Yes, especially the dreams. They're all jumbled up, like in the movie." Very jumbled up, she thought, picturing Brady naked in the hot tub.

The guys returned, and Clare picked up a second video. "I'd like to watch *Regarding Henry*. My therapist talked about it."

Brady frowned. "Are you sure, Clare? None of us has seen that one. I don't want it to upset you."

"I'll be fine."

But she wasn't. It became clear only ten minutes into the film that Harrison Ford, aka Henry, was a jerk. He was a workaholic and neglected his family; his treatment of his daughter was especially abhorrent. It also became clear that both he and his wife had had affairs. The plot revolved around Henry getting shot and losing all memory—procedural, episodic and even semantic. Then he turned into a lovable, kind, sensitive human being.

Throughout the beginning of the movie, Clare had felt the emotion build. At one scene, where his daughter is teaching him to read, she couldn't hold back the tears.

Finally Brady looked over, said, "Aw shit," and told Max to turn off the video. Dragging her into his arms, he kissed her head as she once again buried her nose in his chest. "Shh, it's okay."

"No, no it isn't. I was like him. I can feel it. You've all hinted at the fact that I was selfish." She clutched at his shirt. "I hate what I'm finding out about myself."

"Oh, Clare…" she heard Delia say.

And Max's strong voice sounded: "I'll be right back. Come with me, Dee."

Clare sensed when they left the room and she and Brady were alone.

"Clare, baby, don't cry." He kissed her hair. Locked a hand at her neck. "Shh."

She just shook her head. "I was an awful person, just like Henry. I abandoned all of you. Now, I'm different, I know I am. But you shouldn't forgive me."

"Clare, there was more to it than that. I was at fault, too."

She drew back and stared up at him. His blue eyes were so bleak it caused more tears to fall and she laid her hands on the gauzy shirt. "I can't believe you did anything to hurt me, ever."

"Not intentionally."

She was so caught up in him—his face, the way his lips formed a frown—that she was only dimly aware of the ringing of the doorbell.

But she heard voices; Max was displeased. "Sure, fine, come on in."

Glancing over to the door, Brady tensed. He drew Clare's head to his chest. "Damn it, just what we need."

From behind, she heard, "What the hell is going on here?"

It took Clare a minute to realize that was Jonathan's voice. She drew back, wiped her face as best she could, gave Brady a long, apologetic look, and rose.

Jonathan was in the foyer. He wore nicely pressed jeans and a collared shirt, looking more casual than she'd ever seen him. But his stance and his expression were anything but relaxed. With barely suppressed anger, he said, "I thought you wanted some time to regroup. To be alone."

"I'm sorry, Jonathan. Actually I wanted some time with my friends. I should have been more specific." She cleared her throat. "More honest."

Brady came up behind her and placed his hands on her

shoulders. "Hey, Jon. We were just watching some movies about amnesia. In light of what happened to Clare."

Jonathan glanced at Brady's proprietary gesture, then at Clare. There was fury in his eyes. "If you'll excuse me," he said and walked out.

Brady squeezed her shoulder. "Let him go. Come back to the movies, babe."

Clare wanted to do that. She wanted to stay with Brady and her friends. But every day she was finding out how she'd abandoned people in the past few years, and even though she couldn't remember the details, she was ashamed of her behavior. "No, I can't let him go like this. I'm sorry."

She walked out the door, but not before she saw the sadness on Delia's face, Max's anger and Brady's pained expression. Damn it, couldn't she do anything without hurting somebody?

JONATHAN TRIED TO KEEP his feelings at bay as he strode down the walkway to his car, but they surfaced anyway. He knew in his gut he was going to lose her to them. He should have known, after what he did, that it would come to this. He wasn't going to get off, after all.

"Jonathan, wait."

Go, he told himself when he heard Clarissa call out. *Don't beg. Don't put yourself through this again.*

But he stopped. Where had all his gumption gone? He loved her so much he was losing a piece of himself in the process. Turning, he watched her walk toward him in the moonlight. The beams kissed her blond hair, and it looked lighter. She wore simple jean capris and a long white top, the outfit making her seem younger than she was. And when she got close, the expression on her face was conflicted. She gestured to the left side of the house. "Come sit over there with me."

A bench graced the lawn and it was a warm June night, warm enough to be outside with your girl. Bitterly, Jonathan wondered if Clarissa would ever truly be his, but he followed her over and sat down. He let the stars twinkle and moon shine on them and tried to reason with himself.

Then, for the first time since the accident, Clarissa touched him of her own volition. She took his hand and held it between the two of hers. "I'm sorry I hurt you tonight. You've been nothing but kind to me for three weeks. You sacrificed your job, everything, for me."

The weight of his hypocrisy was almost too much to bear. "I wanted to do that."

She waited a bit, then spoke again. "Jonathan, I don't know how to say this without hurting you even more, but I have to get it out in the open. I want to be with you, but I need to spend time with my friends, too. I..." She glanced around. "I can't believe I'm the type of person who doesn't. They're wonderful people. And surely you and I couldn't have been together constantly, even every night."

"No. But, honey, you don't remember this—you grew apart from those three in there. You didn't have much in common with them anymore. I swear you haven't been to movie night in at least six months." All of that, at least, was the truth.

"What a shame, then. It was fun... Well, until the last part."

He tried to forget the image of her cuddled up to Langston, but he couldn't. What that scenario resurrected for him was even harder to banish. Again he felt utter rage well up inside him. He knew it was in his voice when he said, "You were in Langston's arms, damn it. Letting him hold you."

"I got upset when we watched *Regarding Henry*."

Jonathan spat out an expletive. "How could they pick that video?"

"No one had seen it. They didn't know what kind of person Henry was and how it related to my situation."

"They did it on purpose, to upset you."

"That's ridiculous."

"How would you know that, Clarissa?"

"I sense they'd never do anything to purposely hurt me."

"You hurt them. Now's their chance to get back at you."

Her hands went to her temples, and she stood abruptly. "This isn't the way I wanted our conversation to go. I didn't come out here to let you bad-mouth my friends."

He was distancing her with his anger, so he quelled it as best he could and drew her back down. "Sit, honey. I'm sorry I'm upsetting you."

Though she was still agitated, she dropped back onto the bench. "I can't figure all this out. Why would I let my friends go? There had to be room in my life for all of you."

"You chose to dedicate yourself to your work. And to me."

"But Brady's part of my work."

How much to say? He could be honest about that, he guessed. And he *was* fighting for his life here. "You and Langston were disagreeing a lot."

"Honestly? I can't imagine that. We seem so close. I remember him on a visceral level."

In a way she didn't remember Jonathan. The thought cut him to the quick, more than seeing her in the guy's arms. Now, he felt desperate. So he pushed. "You were making plans to syndicate the show, hopefully with the Cooking

Channel. And as I told you before, the cookbooks would be secondary."

"He put his career on hold for my cookbooks, and then I was going to leave him behind?" She shook her head, sending waves of hair around her face. "No wonder he was mad."

"Did he tell you that?"

"No, I read all his children's books today. They are exceptional."

"Ah. While I thought you were resting."

Clarissa sighed heavily. "Jonathan, I'm not accountable to you for how I spend my time. Surely it's not an unreasonable request to be with my friends and work alone with Brady when need be."

"Just so you're not accountable to *him*, either." That statement caused another spurt of guilt.

"I'd like to be accountable to myself! And for everybody to let me do that."

He raked a hand through his hair. "I'm sorry. I...I just don't want to lose you to them."

"I don't understand that concern."

"Clarissa, you and I, we aren't as close as we were before the accident. And it makes me feel bad."

She went very still. "Do you mean physically again?"

"Partly. And then I come here and see Langston all over you. How do you think that makes me feel?"

"Bad, and I'm sorry, but it was a brotherly hug." Her face, though, flushed. He wished to God he didn't know why.

"Just remember, honey, it was you and I who were sleeping together for over a year."

Subtly, she inched away.

"No, don't do that. I won't pressure you for more. But look at this from my side. I miss being with you, as much as we were before, and how we were before. Can't you understand that?"

"I guess I can. But you shouldn't have come over tonight when I asked you not to. You wouldn't have seen what you did and misinterpreted it if you hadn't been presumptuous."

"Presumptuous? I was worried! I couldn't reach you."

Again, she stood. "I'm exhausted. I'm going inside."

He rose, too. "Can I come up?"

"Jonathan, didn't you hear what I said? I need some space. I'm going back to my friends. I'll call you tomorrow."

Because he wanted badly to hold her, he stepped forward. She stepped back, and the look on her face told him that a hug was the last thing *she* wanted. So, curtly, he said, "Fine."

He watched her leave. Climb the steps. Open the door. Let herself inside.

Damn, damn, damn. Langston had his claws in her again. Nothing Jonathan had done since the accident, or before that, had changed anything. Langston was winning the silent battle for Clarissa that, for a very long time, he and Jonathan had been waging.

No, Jonathan told himself as he headed for the car. *I won't let that happen*. Not after getting a second chance.

So when he got in his Jag, he took out his Palm Pilot and called up his to do list for tomorrow. On the top of it, he put "Contact the Cooking Channel."

THEY WERE STANDING IN the kitchen as if they were at a funeral, drinking beer, mourning their loss. Again. They'd begun to get the old Clare back; even Max was warming up to her. And then she took off with Harris. Just like that, she left them. Brady shouldn't be surprised, but he was—

and the pain she caused him now, a second time, was almost intolerable.

"I told you, bro." Max leaned up against his counter and crossed his arms. "I told you to protect yourself."

"I know." The words stuck in Brady's throat.

"She's probably up there—" Max motioned to the second floor "—with him right now, f—"

"Stop it, Max." This from Delia, who stood by a set of French doors leading to the yard. "She's confused. She's scared. Anybody can see that."

"I'm right here, too." They turned to the doorway and Brady was shocked to see Clare standing there.

Max and Delia were chagrined. They spoke simultaneously.

"Clare, I—"

"Clare, we—"

"Don't apologize for what I overheard. I take it I planned things with you, then canceled them for Jonathan."

Only Max responded in the affirmative.

"Well, that's over. I'm taking control of my life as it is now, even if I don't remember the past. I'm going on my gut." She raised her chin. "I wanted to come tonight, and I wanted to come back in to finish the movies. If you're still willing to give me a chance, that is."

Delia said, "Of course."

"Max?"

"As I said, girl, the jury's still out." He shrugged. "But what the hell, you came back. That's a start."

She focused on Brady. "How about you?"

Silence. What was he to say? It's okay you broke my heart? It's okay I lost my best friend? It's okay I blew everything? He wondered briefly how much longer he could conceal his part in her accident. He faced the others. "Could I have a minute alone with Clare?"

"Sure. We'll go in the living room." Max picked up the pan of brownies. "With these."

"Don't eat them all before we get there," Clare called out. "I know I like chocolate."

When they were alone, Clare wrapped her arms around her waist and stared up at him. "This isn't going to be good, is it?"

"No."

"I...I thought you wanted things to be like they were before, more than any of them." She frowned. "Brady, I *know* that's true, I feel it."

He peeled the label off his beer with his thumbnail. Now that he'd gotten her alone, he was losing his nerve. "It's all true." He looked over at her. "But, Clare, there's something you don't know. I think it's time to bring it out in the open."

"What?"

"Something about the night of the accident."

"You know why I had the accident?"

"Let's just say I know what went on the evening before it. You were here, with me. We argued. Badly."

"Over what?"

"You moving out. We said some nasty things to each other. After...a while, you left upset."

"I was moving out? Where?"

"Into a fancy house with Harris."

Her face flushed. "Why hasn't anybody told me this before?"

"We didn't want to bombard you with information."

"But you could have told me you knew why I left. All you said was you'd seen me early in the evening."

"The truth is, Clare, I was afraid to tell you too much." And he was still afraid to tell her too much. How pathetic.

Clare watched him with wide eyes. Then she shook her head. "All right, if this is true, if this was the cause of my amnesia, shouldn't your telling me this trigger something? It doesn't." She winced. "But I am getting a headache."

"Maybe it'll take a while to sink in." He couldn't keep the desperation out of his voice. When his comments did resonate with her, would she abandon him again?

Goddamn it. He crossed to her and placed his hand over her heart. It was beating like a drum. "You're upset. You should be. You know that I've hurt you, and you don't want to remember it."

Suddenly, she wrapped her arms around his neck and pressed close to him. His body, without his consent, hardened. He regretted that she'd feel his erection, but there was no way he could push her away. And besides, when she remembered, she'd find out his feelings for her had become more than friendly a long time ago. He grasped onto her tightly and buried his face in her neck.

"I have to think about this, Brady. Meanwhile, don't leave me." She nosed into his chest. "Please."

Did he want anything more in his life than to hear those words? Did he want anything more than to have her clinging to him like this?

So he took the coward's way out, as he had in the hospital when he realized she didn't remember most of that night. "Of course I won't leave you." He smoothed down her hair and held her against his chest, wishing he could meld her to him. "Not unless you ask me to."

Which, when her memory returned, she very well might do.

CHAPTER NINE

FOR CLARE, IT HAD BEEN an exhausting and disconcerting week. First, movie night had been a debacle. Torn between Brady and Jonathan, Clare felt as if she hadn't done anything right. Then, Brady had confessed that he and Clare had had an argument the evening of her accident and he believed that had sent her out into the night. She accepted that they'd fought—she had vague recollections of his anger over her moving out—but she didn't accept that the argument had caused her psychological amnesia. Tired of trying to figure it out, which brought on more severe headaches, she and Brady had decided to table the whole thing for now and let her memory return gradually, as the doctors had instructed. It still angered her that no one had told her about her plans to move out, but she had to let that go, too.

She'd also been trying to placate Jonathan all week. In the end, she'd agreed to tape a show. Though it was the last thing she wanted to be doing—she didn't feel ready for such a big step—Jonathan had insisted she try it. After their disagreement on movie night, she felt compelled to make the gesture.

So they entered the studio together at 9:00 a.m.

"Don't be nervous," he said gently, leading her by the elbow. "You look lovely."

She smoothed down the green silk she wore and smiled. "Thanks."

"You'll be fine."

"I'm terrified. I hope I can keep it from the audience that I don't remember a thing about the set or the show."

"You'll do fine," he reiterated. "And it's a tape, so we can stop any time and edit later. Ready?"

"I guess so."

After greeting the staff, who seemed very supportive, she went to the kitchen set and took her place behind the counter. When the music she remembered from watching the show with Brady began, her spirits lightened. She smiled out at the camera pretending she knew where she was and what she was doing.

"Welcome to *Clarissa's Kitchen*. Today we're going to make minestrone soup, one of my favorite dishes." She'd chosen the meal from volume one because she felt safer with older memories. "Accompanying it, we'll have Caesar salad, homemade bread and custard cannoli." She pointed to the several bowls at her left that the prep cooks had done ahead of time. "Start by cleaning and cutting the vegetables." The camera panned on the carrots, celery, escarole and green beans. "Escarole is my favorite choice for this soup, but people use cabbage, too." She smiled engagingly at the camera. "But then it wouldn't be Aunt Joan's recipe."

As she cooked, she talked about the soup and real memories flooded back to her. Clare simply knew many details: her cousins, Stacey, Eric and Katie, all near her age, sneaking raw carrots or a bean. Cathy was with them, too. Watching by the stove as Aunt Joan combined the garlic, onions and potatoes creating the mixture's tart, tangy smell. When the five kids got bored, they went outside to play in the snow, but the pièce de résistance was tromping back in to have a bowl of the steaming soup set in front of them. Then Aunt Joan would grate Romano cheese from a block and finish off their lunch with warm Italian bread.

"Cut." The director had come forward, startling Clare. "Clarissa, are you all right?"

"Huh?"

"You stopped after a few minutes and just stared at the frying pan."

She raised her hands to her cheeks. "Oh dear, I'm sorry."

Jonathan, who'd been hovering in the wings like a mother hen, approached. His expression was concerned, tinged with something else. Fear, maybe? "A memory?"

"Yeah, a good one. When I was little. It was about my aunt making the soup."

"I'm glad," he said, but he didn't sound like he meant it.

And for the first time, as she watched him, Clare suspected Jonathan didn't want her memory to return.

She could only wonder why.

CLARE LOOKED IN THE MIRROR of her vanity and, even four weeks after the accident, still found a stranger, but one she was getting used to, one she was comfortable with. That person preferred wearing the cotton peach capris and matching sleeveless top with sandals she'd put on today more than the clothes she'd had to wear when they'd taped another episode of *Clarissa's Kitchen*. This morning, she was dressed casually because she was going out with Brady.

"Hey, Clare, you ready?" As if her thoughts had conjured him, Brady's voice sounded from the foyer. He'd been coming in without knocking again.

There had been other proof of their closeness, like this

one, since his confession—a touch on her shoulder, a natural grasp of her hand. Obviously he was more at ease with her. Was it because he'd been carrying around so much guilt?

"In here," she called out. It was intimate inviting him into her bedroom, but again the request seemed natural.

He strolled to the doorway. "Hi, there." He kissed her cheek.

She liked it. A lot. Which was an issue, because the day she'd made him frittata hadn't been the only time she'd been aroused by his nearness. Her physical reaction had increased with their easy affection. She'd begun to notice little things— how certain jeans gloved his butt, how a shirt she bought him brought out the blue of his eyes, how virile he seemed when he was sweaty and flushed from working out. This attraction to him had to be inappropriate, given her relationship with Jonathan, but how did a person control such an innate thing?

Leaning against the wall, Brady crossed his arms over a chest covered with a navy T-shirt with Van Gogh's *Sunflowers* on it. He wore it with khaki cargo shorts and sandals. "You look pretty in that outfit."

"Thanks. I like the casual style better."

"But you don't need the makeup."

She caught his gaze in the mirror as she held on to the mascara wand. Ludicrously she remembered Lucinda's perfectly done up face. "I don't?"

"Nah. You're a natural beauty." He ruffled her hair. "It's longer."

"I like it. Jonathan wanted to trim it for the show, but I said no." Despite his comment, she swiped on some mascara and lipstick and stood. "I'm excited about today."

"Thanks for thinking of this, Clare." His voice was filled

with husky gratitude. Briefly she wondered if that's how it got after sex. "Mom is so excited. She gets lonely since Dad died, even though three of her kids are still in Rockford and visit all the time."

"You miss him, don't you?"

"Yeah. He was your typical firefighter—dry humor, kept to himself—but he took us boys to baseball games and never refused to chauffeur the girls to the mall."

"He sounds like a terrific guy."

"Anyway, Mom's going to love working on this part of the book with us."

She frowned. "I feel bad for not suggesting it before. How could I have never thought to do this?"

When they were in need of ten more recipes, and Clare had balked at using ones from her previous books, she'd had a brainstorm.

"LET'S HAVE A SECTION for you."

"For me? I don't cook."

"But your family does. Your mom in particular."

"And?"

"We could call the last ten recipes The Langstons' Kitchen. We can get recipes from your mom, along with any anecdotes you or she or your sisters remember about the food. And just think, you can sketch your own family."

WHEN BRADY HAD GOTTEN moisture in his eyes at her suggestion, she'd felt even worse that she hadn't thought of this before.

With his arm casually slung over her shoulders, they left the house. When they reached the garage, he asked, "Your car or mine?"

This week, she'd also begun driving her little Miata—which Brady had seen to getting fixed after the accident—and found she knew the mechanics. But being behind the wheel made her nervous because she was swamped by associations with the accident, and because she couldn't remember the layout of all the streets. "No. You live out in the suburbs and it means expressway driving. I'm not sure I want to tackle that."

His eyes crinkled at the corners. "Clare, you remembered where I grew up. I haven't told you anything about my house in the past month."

"I did the same thing at the show taping. It seems like the memories are coming back fast." She squeezed his arm. "Maybe I'll remember more when I get to your house."

She did. She recognized the big gray structure and had a quick flashback of going up to Brady's old room and catching a glimpse of his life as a teenager—rock posters, sketches by Dalí and other artists, awards he won in school for his art. She also recalled the backyard, where she had pushed Samantha's child in a swing and where a hammock that Brady favored was strung. And she remembered Lillian Langston as soon as she saw the still-young sixty-year-old waiting on the porch. Though Brady's mother looked tired when they reached her, wonderful, positive emotions welled inside Clare at the sight of this woman.

"There she is." Lillian stepped forward and took Clare in a warm embrace. "It's been a long time, dear."

Clare inhaled the scent of Brady's mom…some kind of bath splash or lotion. "Oh!"

Lillian pulled back. "What, Clare?"

"Your lotion—you gave me some for Christmas one

year." She took in an excited breath. "I remember spending Christmas here when Cathy couldn't come for the holidays."

"You spent a few with us." She peered at Clare with Brady's eyes, a deep blue. "Good memories, I hope."

"The best. Thank you for opening your home to me."

"You enjoyed the fuss," Lillian said, leading Clare inside. "All my children and their kids came home. I was afraid it would be too much for you."

"I always wanted a big family." She halted. "Oh, Lord. I did." She turned to Brady, who'd followed them in. "Things are coming back so fast."

His frown came quickly. "Is it too much?"

"No, just a bit startling."

They went directly to the kitchen, where Lillian had her recipe box out and several cards spread across the table. "Can I get you something, dear?"

"No, thanks. I ate breakfast."

"Honey?" Her gaze rested on her son with such love, such deep emotion, Clare's heart did a little lurch. She had only vague recollections of her parents, and that made her feel bad.

"I'll get some coffee. You sit with Clare."

Lillian touched the box. "I hope it's all right—I picked out some recipes. More than ten, so you can choose from them."

Clare sat down and scanned the cards. "Brady, come over here. I want to know your favorites. Maybe ones with stories attached—though, Lillian, you might have anecdotes he doesn't."

Carrying his coffee mug, Brady crossed to stand behind Clare. This time, *his* scent surrounded her. She was hit by a powerful urge to lean back, take his arms and encircle her chest with them, kiss the bare skin on his arm, his knuckles.

Obviously unaware of her reaction, Brady chuckled as

he looked at each card, nicely printed as if his mother had rewritten them. "Elephant ears? I was what, Mom, five when we made them?"

"Yes, and you cried when I first suggested them. You were scared we'd use real elephants."

"Elephant-ear cookies it is," Clare said, plucking out the card.

He also picked a homemade pudding and related the story of how his mother used to let him pudding paint—a sort of finger paint that you could eat and play with.

"I think I have a picture of Brady at three covered with chocolate."

"Brady, you could draw that."

"If I recall, I was in a diaper," he said dryly.

"The readers will love it."

They picked one more dessert, chocolate ice cream roll, and went on to main dishes. Brady had liked Spanish rice, fried chicken, baked ziti with cheese only and a specially spiced cider that he once poured over his head.

"I have a photo of that, too," Lillian said, laughing.

"Why don't you go get some of the pictures, Lillian? Brady can decide which might be easiest to base a drawing on."

As she stood, Brady's mother's face was alight. "This is so much fun. Thanks for including me."

She squeezed Lillian's arm. "I'm glad. Let me say I'm sorry I didn't think of using your recipes sooner."

"It's never too late, dear." She started to move away but grabbed on to the edge of the table. "Oh."

"Mom?"

"I'm a little short of breath." Lillian waited. "It's gone now."

Brady's face darkened with concern and he grasped her arm. "Has this happened before?"

"Only in the past couple of weeks. I talked to one of the doctors at the hospital. He said it could be anything and ran a few tests, but nothing showed up."

"Why didn't you tell me about this?" Brady's tone was stern.

"Because you'd worry. Like you are now. But hush, because I'm having so much fun."

When Lillian went to the living room, Brady dropped down into a chair next to Clare. Anxiety practically radiated from him. "I hate that. Any time she doesn't feel well."

"The love between you two is so palpable, Brady."

His eyes were worried.

"If the symptom continues, you should follow up with her and her doctors."

"Yeah." He put his hand over hers. "She's loving every minute of this."

"So am I."

"Embarrassing me is fun, woman?"

"I know you. You'll get a kick out of drawing yourself when you were young. Put in some others—your mom, Samantha, Juliana, Sloan and Peter."

"You remember my siblings' names."

"Oh, Lord. I do. Brady, how come? Why do I remember your family so well?"

Lifting his hand, he brushed his knuckles down her cheek. She leaned into the caress.

"Clare, love—"

A crash sounded from the living room, drawing them both out of the moment. Brady bolted up and Clare hurried behind him.

THE AMBULANCE SIREN SCREAMED around them, making Brady's teeth hurt. He'd grasped his mother's hand in his and held on tightly. They were cramped in the small space, but Brady didn't care. "You're okay, Mom. We're almost there."

"BP 170 over 96." The female attendant looked up at Brady because his mother was semiconscious. "Has it always been this high?"

"I don't think so. C-could it be a stroke?"

"I don't know, sir." Her voice was kind. "You said you found her clutching her chest, so the attack could be heart-related."

He groaned and felt Clare's hand on his back. "There's help here," she said. "She's getting good care."

Glancing over his shoulder, he thought briefly of how he'd been taking care of this woman for a month. Now she was the strong one, more like her old self before the amnesia.

The attendant added, "It's good that you called the ambulance within minutes of the attack."

That, too, had been Clare's doing. When they'd burst into the living room and found his mother collapsed on the floor in front of the bookshelf full of photo albums, Brady had frozen. Clare had called 9-1-1, drawn him back when the ambulance came and badgered their way into riding with his mother.

It seemed an eternity before they arrived at Memorial Hospital where, ironically, his mother worked. At the emergency entrance, the sirens stopped abruptly, and Brady and Clare bounded out of the ambulance. The crew got his mother out and wheeled her inside.

"Go on over to the desk, Mr. Langston," the attendant said kindly. "You'll need to fill out forms."

Immobilized, Brady stared at the doors to the E.R. treatment area as they closed.

Clare linked her arm with his. "Come on, Brade, let's do what the attendant said."

She escorted him to the desk. A nurse turned around. "Hey, Brady, hi."

Brady frowned. "I'm sorry I…"

"Janice Carson. I've worked with your mom for years." She reached over and squeezed his arm. "I promise she'll receive the best attention. We all adore her. And I'll get word to you as quickly as I can."

Feeling as if he were in a dream, Brady just stood there.

Janice held up a clipboard. "Can you fill these out now?"

When Brady didn't take the forms, Clare did. "Yes, we'll be over there." She led him to the sitting area where cushioned double-seaters faced each other.

Brady dropped down beside her on one. "I…I'll do that."

"No, I will. I'll just ask you questions."

"I don't know stuff. Her insurance…"

Clare held up a black bag he recognized as his mother's purse. "It was in the foyer on a table. I grabbed it as we left."

Dazed, Brady stared at his mother's bag and felt moisture well in his eyes. "When I was little and jealous of the most recent addition to our family, Mom would send me to get something in her purse and I'd find candy or gum or some other surprise there." He swallowed hard. "She put them there just for me so I'd know how special I was to her."

"That sounds like Lillian."

"Clare, I…I'm not sure I can do this." He gestured to the hospital. "All of this. What if something happens to her? Like my dad?"

"It's hard waiting. But let's not borrow trouble."

She began filling out the forms, and answering the questions distracted him. There was still no word when they finished. Clare tried to reassure him. "It's only been twenty minutes."

"Should I call my sisters and brothers?"

"It might be best to wait until we have some news."

"You're probably right." He rose and walked to the window. He was staring out at the busy city street when he felt her come up behind him. She slid her arms around him from the back but said nothing. Her embrace felt good, made him stronger. Then she came to his side, linked their arms and stared outdoors with him. Rockford motorists and pedestrians were following their normal routines while Brady's life was falling apart.

"She's always been so strong. So *there* for all of us. When Dad died, she was everybody's rock. Mine especially, because I fell apart."

"It's all right to fall apart. You love your mother. Showing fear is okay." She laid her head against his shoulder. "I think you told me that once."

They continued the vigil for twenty more minutes and then the desk nurse, Janice, approached them. "Brady, Dr. Nichols is coming out…here he is now."

A tall, dark-haired man in blue scrubs came up to them. Brady had met him once. "Brady." The doctor's face was lined with concern.

Brady grabbed for Clare's hand.

"We're pretty sure Lillian has had a heart attack. We're going to prep her for an angiogram now."

"Don't you need to do tests? Check the blood enzymes?" Max's father had had a heart attack and Brady knew the procedure.

"We ran one, but we're not waiting for the results of a second. She's got the classic symptoms. And I don't want to waste any time."

"Oh my God."

Dr. Nichols's gaze was sympathetic. "We've got the best cardio team in the city. And we all care about your mother. Everyone's dropping everything to do this."

"Thank you," Clare said when Brady didn't speak.

"You'll need to sign consent forms, since you're listed as power of attorney."

"I—I will. Dr. Nichols, tell me the truth. It's bad, isn't it?"

"It's serious, hence the way we're proceeding. I'll be back out once we do the angiogram."

Brady turned to Clare after he left. "I can't believe it."

"Heart surgery is so advanced today. A guy at the station had quintuple bypass and is playing golf, doing everything he did before."

"It's my *mother*."

"I know." She fished in her purse and pulled out her cell phone. "I think you need to call your brothers and sisters."

"I do? I *do*?"

"Yes, Brady, you do."

The tears slipped down his cheeks. The next thing he knew, he was in Clare's arms, crying like a baby.

THE NEWS OF THE NEED for double bypass surgery for Lillian Langston came after Juliana, Samantha and Sloan—who had driven from two hours away—had all arrived at the hospital. Once again, Brady took the verdict the worst. And once again, he turned to Clare, and not his sisters or brothers, to console him.

They were in a smaller, more private waiting area, and

Brady sat staring at the floor, gripping Clare's hand so hard it hurt. The surgery had begun at 8:00 p.m. and it was nine now.

"Hey," Sloan said, coming over to his brother. The boys looked alike with the same dark hair, blue eyes and even the same square-cut jaw. "You okay, buddy?"

Brady looked up at his younger brother and the expression in his eyes was so bleak it broke Clare's heart. "No. Sorry I'm such a wimp."

"You were always the worst," Juliana, Samantha's twin, commented. She was sitting on the other side of Brady and slid her arm around his shoulders. She and Sam were identical, though they'd cut their dark hair differently, and Juliana was a bit more slender. "Remember when Mom had her appendix out? Dad had to let you sleep with him."

"I never lived that down," Brady said, trying to joke. He drew in a breath. "I don't…" He turned to Clare and rested his forehead on her shoulder.

Clare clasped his neck. From over his shoulders, she saw the siblings exchange glances. So what? Maybe she hadn't been here for Brady before, but she was here now.

Her phone vibrated. She'd been trying to reach Max, who was off on another trip, and Delia, who'd gone to join Donny at his grandparents' house. She drew her phone out and, against hospital rules, answered it.

"Clare, I've been calling you all day." Jonathan's tone was impatient, irritated. But Clare recognized the fear in his voice, too.

"Is it Max or Delia?" Brady asked.

Into the phone, she said, "Just a sec." To Brady, "No. I'm going to step out in the hall and take this."

Panic filled Brady's face. "Don't go."

"I won't. I promise. I'll be in the hall, away from the nurses."

Sam took her place and Clare went into a private alcove where she wouldn't be seen by the phone police. "Jonathan, I'm back."

"Honey, where are you? You've been out of reach all day. Didn't you get my messages?"

"I did. I'm sorry. I've been at the hospital since this morning."

"Oh, Lord. Did something happen to you? Why didn't you call me?"

"No, it's not me. It's Brady's mother." She explained the situation.

"I'm sorry to hear that." A very long pause. "So you've been there all day? And rode in the ambulance?"

"Yes."

"Why don't I come and get you? You must be exhausted. You're not fully recovered, you know."

A spurt of anger shot through her. How could he possibly suggest she abandon Brady at a time like this? "I can't leave, Jonathan."

There was another long pause on his end, then he asked, "Are the Langston sisters and brothers there?"

"All but Peter. He's flying in from the west coast."

"Well, there you go."

"Jonathan, I have no intention of leaving the hospital. Lillian's still in surgery. And Max and Delia aren't in town."

Another pause. "I'm sorry if I sound insensitive. But I've got great news. The Cooking Channel has agreed to see us tomorrow at four. They've had a cancellation, and we got the time slot. I want you rested for that."

She struggled to control her temper. She hadn't agreed

to pursue the syndication of the show, had told Jonathan how wary she was of starting something new with huge gaps in her memory. He said she just didn't remember how important this was to her, but hell, even taping her show was foreign to her. She wasn't ready to pursue her career even further. And she resented him for pushing her too hard.

"You'll have to reschedule. I can't go."

"Lillian will be out of surgery in a few hours. They'll know her prognosis then. Stay if you must, but we have to catch a plane tomorrow at noon."

A nurse walked by her. "I'm sorry, ma'am. Cell phones aren't allowed. I suspect you know… Oh, you're with the Langstons?" Clare nodded. "Go ahead then, dear." She continued walking.

"Jonathan, the nurse just came by and told me to get off my cell. I'll call you when I know more."

Before he could respond, she clicked off.

When she turned, she saw Brady behind her in the hallway. His face was completely devoid of color, and his whole body was as tense as a tree limb about to snap. A swell of sympathy, and something else very big and very powerful, filled her.

"Who was it?" he asked.

"Jonathan. He said to give you his best."

"Yeah, sure."

"Do you want to go get coffee or something?"

"Should I?"

"I think that would be good." She checked her watch. "It'll be hours yet before the surgery is over."

"A nurse came in while you were out here and said it's going well. Mom's stable and they haven't found anything they weren't expecting."

"That's wonderful. Come on, let's go get coffee and maybe some food in your stomach. You need that, Brady."

He grasped her hand. "I need you. Here. Promise me you'll stay."

Once again, so much emotion for this man filled her. "I'll stay. I promise."

Hand in hand, they found the elevator and took it to the cafeteria. She might not have her memory back, but one thing Clare knew for sure: she meant what she said. She was going to stay with Brady as long as he needed her.

AT TEN THE NEXT MORNING, carrying a suit Clarissa had left at his house, Jonathan entered Memorial Hospital and took the elevator to the cardiac waiting area. He'd spoken briefly to her earlier. She'd stayed all night with the Langstons, but thankfully, Lillian had come through the surgery and was in recovery, and her children had visited her in CCU. Now that all was well, Clarissa could go with him.

What he found in the waiting area made his throat tight. All of them were there—the Langston girls were asleep on couches, and the men were awake. Two were leafing through magazines, but Brady was staring down at Clarissa, who was sound asleep, with her head cradled on a pillow in his lap. His hand was absently stroking her hair. The small gesture made Jonathan angry and resurrected a jealousy buried deep inside him, but he tried not to let either emotion show because of the gravity of the situation.

"Hello," one of the Langston brothers said when he spotted Jonathan. "Are you looking for someone?"

"Clarissa."

Brady glanced up. His face was lined with fatigue and remnants of worry, and Jonathan felt bad for the guy.

Though his own parents were still alive, he did remember how his grandfather had gone through heart bypass and how difficult the aftermath had been.

"Hi, Brady. I'm sorry to hear about your mother and glad she's come through the surgery."

"What are you doing here?"

"I've come to get Clarissa. She's got to change—" he held up the garment bag "—for our trip to New York."

"Clare's not going anywhere."

"She said she'd stay until your mother was out of danger." He tried to keep his tone gentle. On some level, he knew he was being selfish, but the prize was too big to let go of. "No new developments, right?"

"My mother's doing okay. What's in New York?"

"The Cooking Channel. They want to see Clarissa about picking up our show. You know how much she wants this."

"I know how much *you* want it."

Again, he curtailed his temper out of respect. Just then, Clarissa stirred. Jonathan watched as she came awake. She yawned, then looked up at Brady. A smile claimed her lips. Then a frown. "What? Brady, you look terrible. Did something happen while I was asleep?"

"*He* happened."

Clarissa looked over at Jonathan, then sat up, raked back her hair and stood. She was a mess—her clothes, her hair, her makeup. "Jonathan, what are you doing here?"

"I came to get you. We can still make our plane to New York." Again he held up the bag. "You said you'd come if everything went well."

"You did?" Brady asked.

Clarissa looked at Jonathan. Then at Brady. She was

deathly still, and Jonathan knew the choice she was about to make would tell him how everything else was going to go down.

BRADY STARED OPENMOUTHED as Clare exited the room with Harris. He couldn't believe she'd leave him now. Dropping down on the chair, he buried his face in his hands, feeling even more bereft than before.

"Brady, I'm sorry." Samantha's voice on the left. Her tone was angry. "You don't need this."

He couldn't respond.

From his right, Juliana rubbed his back and leaned her head on his shoulder. "We're here, Brade. It's okay."

He guessed it had to be, since the writing, so to speak, was on the wall. And this time he wasn't going to justify Clare's choice of Jonathan over him. This time he wasn't going to fool himself into thinking things were different.

"Oh," Sam said.

Brady didn't move at her exclamation. He wanted to shut out the world.

Jules nudged him. "Brady."

Sighing, he raised his head. And frowned. "What? What's going on?"

Clare stood in the doorway. She gave him a half smile. "I'm not flying to New York with Jonathan. I was fuzzy from sleep or I wouldn't have gone out the door with him in the first place." She came closer, dropped to her knees and grasped his hands. "I may have gone back on my word in the past, but I'm not doing it again. I'm here for you, Brady, for as long as you need me."

Her tone was so sincere that Brady wanted badly to believe her. "You promise?"

She smiled up at him. "Yes. And it's a promise I'll keep."

CHAPTER TEN

HIS HANDS WERE MAGIC on her body. Clare sighed as he kneaded her breasts, kissed the swell of each one, closed his mouth over a nipple.

"Ahh," she moaned, clasping his head to keep him where he was. His dark hair curled at his neck, and she weaved her fingers through it.

"I knew you'd like this."

Again, she moaned.

He slid his palm down her rib cage, over her stomach, and cupped her. His mouth followed the trail.

"Oh, oh, Brady…"

Clare awoke with a start. Disoriented, she glanced around the room and checked the other side of the bed. The covers were jumbled and a pillow lay on the floor, but she was alone. Her heart racing, her body taut, she realized she was seriously aroused.

"Hell!" she murmured, lying back on the pillow and pushing her hair out of her face. The fan whirred above her and she watched the white blades go round. "What was that all about?"

You know, Clare. Be honest with yourself.

All right, she *did* know the answer to her question. Over the past week, she'd spent all her time with Brady, both at the hospital and one night back at the condo when he'd slept in her bed with her, though they were both fully clothed. Even in the three days since Lillian had come home, and Brady had been staying at his mom's, Clare had gone over during the day. She kept him company, cooked for them both and froze food for later. She entertained Lillian by asking for stories about the recipes, so Brady could take a break or run errands.

All the while, something had grown between her and Brady. Whether they were old feelings resurrected or new ones blossoming, Clare felt closer to him than to anyone else; she treasured the fact that she was able to help him and she relished her time with him. It was almost like...falling in love.

The thought stunned her. They were friends. Best friends.

Then why, she asked herself as she flung back the covers, did she crave his touch, want to feel his skin beneath her hands, yearn for him to give her more than a peck on the cheek? There must be more to what she was feeling, and today she'd talk to her therapist about it. She had an appointment in two hours.

The phone rang as she finished her shower. Wrapped in a thirsty red towel, her hair damp, she answered it.

"Hey, Clare."

"Hi, Cathy. There's nothing wrong, is there?"

"No. I'm just leaving Arizona. I should be in Rockford at four."

"I'll be waiting at the airport."

"I can take a cab."

"No way. See you then."

More positive feelings filled her. Cathy was coming to spend a week with her. They were going to be together— like old times, her sister had said—and it delighted Clare.

She'd just hung up the phone when it rang again. "Hello."

"Hello, Clarissa." Jonathan's voice, cold and distant on the other end. He'd been this way all week because she'd insisted he cancel the New York trip, and because she hadn't seen him in four days. She recalled now that he often distanced himself when he was hurt. The knowledge softened her attitude toward him. "Are you well?" he asked.

"Yes." A pause. "Are you?"

"No, of course not. I'd like to see you."

She hedged. "Cathy's coming today."

"It would be nice to finally meet her."

"You've never met my sister?"

"Ah, no, you didn't see much of her in the last year, when we were dating seriously."

Guilt swamped Clare, dousing all the positive feelings she'd just experienced. She hadn't seen her sister in a year? She'd been told they were estranged, but this much?

"Clarissa?"

Another kind of guilt made her remember all Jonathan had done for her. His comment about Cathy reminded Clare how she had abandoned a lot of people in the past, and it was time to turn that around. So she said, "Why don't you come to dinner tomorrow night? I'll cook your favorite meal."

"That would be great." He sounded relieved. And pleased.

"Um, Jonathan, what *is* your favorite?"

A pause. "Your Chicken Cordon Bleu."

"Oh, good." Silence. "I'm sorry about not being able to see you all week." Which was only partly true.

"I understand. Langston's needs came first."

"His mother—"

"No, honey, don't. We aren't going to fight about this again."

He'd lost his temper in the hall at the hospital, as he did about anything concerning her time with Brady. Clare had accused him of being selfish, and he'd left in a huff when she declared she was staying with the Langstons. She hated hurting him, but down deep it felt right to be making her own decisions again.

He added, "We can work through this. We can work through anything."

Clare had a blinding flash of him saying that to her before, but it was gone before she could remember where or when. And it wasn't a good memory. It made her feel cold again.

"Then I'll see you tomorrow at around seven."

Another pause. "I love you, Clarissa."

Oh, damn. He hadn't said those words to her since she'd awakened from the coma. Another memory came, Jonathan's voice loud and clear...

I love you, Clarissa... I've always loved you... This doesn't change anything.

Her head began to pound. Not another headache. She hadn't had one all week and willed the pain back. "I care about you, too, Jonathan." She couldn't manage more. "I have to go. I'll see you tomorrow night."

Dropping down on the bed, she sat there immobile for a few seconds. Running her hand across the quilt, she shook her head. She'd dreamed Brady was making love to her. Yet, Jonathan told her today—and in the past, obviously— that he loved her. And Brady said she had been planning to move in with Jonathan, for God's sake. Why couldn't she remember the course of events that led to her accident?

She became even more agitated on the drive over to the hospital for her therapy appointment, thinking about

Brady and the dream the whole way. By the time Anna Summers opened her office door and Clare stepped inside, she was a wreck.

As soon as she sat, Anna gave her a once-over. "You're upset. More memories?"

"Who the hell knows what they are?"

A sympathetic smile. "It's common to get frustrated when the past comes back in pieces, incomplete and confusing. But the good news is that things *are* coming back, and that means your memory is returning. My guess is it won't be too much longer until you have the whole picture."

She stared at Anna. "I'm not sure I want the whole picture anymore."

"Why?"

"Anna, something's not right in my life. I dreamed last night that Brady was making love to me."

"Hmm. You are close. Unusually close for being only friends."

"But we *are* just friends."

"As I said before, dreams aren't a reflection of reality, Clare. Or even what you want reality to be. These particular ones could be manifesting the closeness you feel toward Brady in a different way."

"But it was so real. I woke…aroused."

"That's understandable, too. You haven't had sex in weeks."

"Wouldn't I want sex with Jonathan?"

"It would seem reasonable."

"I don't. I don't feel attracted to him, today in the present."

"And before you were?"

"He says I was. And surely, if we've been together for over a year, we've made love. He said as much."

"I don't doubt that."

She tugged at the hem of her blouse, a nervous gesture that didn't seem at all familiar. "Why is this happening? With Brady? It's affecting how I feel when I'm with him."

"Maybe you were always attracted to him on some level and just suppressed it. Maybe he feels that, too."

"Why wouldn't we have acted on it? We've been friends for ten years."

"I'm not sure. Could you ask him about it?"

"I usually feel like I could ask him anything. But his mother just came home from the hospital, and I don't want to upset him."

"For what it's worth, looking at this psychologically, it seems to me you're closer to Brady than to Jonathan."

"All my friends, including Brady, say I wasn't close to any of them anymore."

"Yes, it does appear contradictory. But that's the nature of amnesia." Anna shrugged. "Did you write down this dream, too?"

"Ah, no."

Anna smiled. "Clare, I'm not a prude."

"Anna, this dream was so hot I'm not sure I can get it down on paper."

They both laughed aloud.

"All right. I'll give you a pass on this one."

Clare sobered. "There's something else, too." She sighed, not wanting to recall the discussion she'd had with Brady on movie night. "Brady thinks he's responsible for my amnesia."

"Why on earth would he think that?"

"He says we had a fight late that night about my moving out."

"You were moving out of the condo?"

"And in with Jonathan."

"Why didn't anyone give you that piece of information before this?"

"Brady said they were following doctors' orders not to reveal too much too soon." She frowned. "He thinks our argument is what sent me into the night."

Anna came to the edge of her seat. "Honestly? Was it right before the accident?"

She nodded. "I think so, but I can't figure out why one more argument with Brady would be enough to cause memory loss. I know we'd been fighting a lot then."

"I'm leaning toward something more happening that night."

"Damn it. Why can't I remember?"

"You're trying too hard. Relax and let it come on its own, as the other memories have."

Clare left her session with Anna feeling vaguely unsatisfied. She got in her car and drove out to the suburbs. To Brady's house. To Brady. She knew the way.

He answered the door barefoot and bare-chested, wearing only low-slung denim shorts. Clare thought she might just swallow her tongue when she saw him. "Hey, there, gorgeous, come on in." His hair was damp from the shower, and his skin gleamed.

She gawked.

"You okay?"

"Um, yeah. Just killing time till Cathy comes."

Tugging her inside, he left the door open to the screen, allowing the warm July air inside. "You must be excited about seeing your sister."

She noticed his chest was a little damp. Droplets nestled in the springy hair there. "Excited?"

"Hey, earth to Clare?"

"Oh, sorry. Yeah, I can't wait to see her. I have a feeling a lot of memories will come back."

There it was again. The wariness in Brady's eyes when her memory returning completely was mentioned. How odd, too, since he'd already confessed what had happened that night.

"Clare, you're spacing out again. Are you sure everything's all right?"

"I don't know. I have a lot to think about."

"I'm here if you want to talk."

She nodded. "I know you are. But I'm not ready yet. I'm anxious to see Cathy, though."

They were still inside the foyer. "Sweetheart, I know I mentioned this before, but you and Cathy haven't been close for a while."

"Jonathan said the same thing this morning. He's never met her."

"You were, um, with Jonathan this morning?" Brady's tone was strained and he was frowning.

"No, I talked to him on the phone before my therapy appointment."

"Oh, good. How did the appointment go?"

"Don't ask." She pushed back her hair. "I feel bad about my estrangement from my own sister. Same old, same old, I guess."

"I hope you aren't disappointed."

"You're sweet to be concerned. Now, can I visit your mom? I thought I might cheer her up by talking about some recipes."

She started down the hall, but he headlocked her from behind, the gesture meant to be playful. When he drew her close, his scent of soap and aftershave just about knocked her off her feet. The last thing she needed now was to be feeling Brady's almost naked body against her.

Still, she closed her eyes and steeped herself in his closeness. His chest was warm, solid, muscled. His scent enveloped her. She felt safe but energized. Cared for but desired.

Desired? Oh, God, just like in the dream.

CLARE HUGGED CATHY AGAIN when they got inside her condo. She'd remembered her sister as soon as she'd come into the arrivals area at the airport. It wasn't a flashback, it wasn't because she'd seen pictures, it was because she *knew* this woman. They were flesh and blood, and her very cells felt the connection. "I'm so glad you came."

Cathy was more petite than Clare, her hair lighter, but their eyes were the same color. She seemed anxious, too, which made Clare sad. "*I'm* so glad you remember me."

"I do. Other than Brady, you're the only person I know intuitively."

Cathy grinned.

"Come on, I'll show you where you can stay." She led Cathy into her office, which had a sofa bed across the room from her desk and bookshelves.

"Are you sure you want me to sleep in here? I won't be in the way?"

"Of course not. Why?"

"Since you started the TV show, you've been pretty protective of your work space. The last time I came to Rockford, I stayed in a hotel."

Like a movie screen showing flashbacks, she saw Cathy openmouthed when Clare had pulled up to a hotel...

You're kidding, right?

Look, Cathy, I've got my stuff spread all over the office. You'll be more comfortable here.

Maybe I shouldn't have come.

Don't start that again. This isn't a big deal...

Clare frowned. "I remember. It's terrible that I made you stay at a hotel. I'm so sorry, Cath."

"Let's forget about that. I'm just happy to be here today."

"I'll let you get settled while I start cooking us some supper."

Clare headed to the kitchen and crossed to the shelf where her cookbooks were. Number five had My Baby Sister's Choice, beef burgundy. Trying to forget what kind of person she'd been to her own flesh and blood, Clare got out the chuck roast she'd bought and cut earlier, and put it on the stove to brown. She also took out the vegetables and began preparing them to add to the dish when she put everything into the oven. The sautéing meat smelled good and she... Oh, sharp pain made Clare step back from the stove and grab her head. Images burst through her brain...

CLARE ON THE PHONE. Dressed for taping a show where she would make beef burgundy. She was tapping her toe on the floor impatiently. "Then leave the bastard. No, Cathy, don't cry. Look, I'm sorry to be so blunt, but he's never been nice enough to you. Yes, I did like him once..."

From the phone came Cathy's voice: "You're cruel sometimes, Clare. You never have time for me or any of your—"

"I'll tell you what I don't have time for—this whining. For God's sake, it isn't the first time he cheated on you. I'd never take that from any man."

"No, of course not, not the great Clarissa Boneli..."

"CLARE?"

She found herself doubled over at the sink, clutching her stomach, unable to bear what she'd just remembered.

"Clare!"

Cathy was at her side. "Come on, sweetie. Oh, God, you're crying. Did you burn yourself?"

Clare couldn't stop the tears. Cathy just held her until finally she quieted. Her sister led her to a chair, then crossed to the sink, got her a glass of water and set it on the table. "What happened?"

"I was cooking the beef burgundy. And I had a horrible, horrible memory."

"Of what?"

"Of talking to you on the phone. You were weeping over…" She thought hard. "Derek."

Cathy's face drained of color. She didn't say anything.

More memories flooded Clare. Cathy's wedding, honeymoon pictures, Clare spending time with them at their apartment in Arizona. And Derek's philandering ways.

"What did you remember?"

"When I told you to leave him. I was impatient and mean to you on the phone. Cath, I was an awful person."

"No, no, sweetie, don't think about it."

"I have to. What I did was unconscionable. How long was I…like that?"

"Things were good until about two years ago. We were close before that."

Again, Clare saw images. Of her and Cathy riding bikes together, holding hands at funerals, cooking with Grandma Boneli, calling each other from college, shopping in New York.

"I remember those times, too." She shook her head. "But I can't believe what kind of person I was."

Cathy seemed much older as she sat down at the table and clasped Clare's hands in hers. "You know what, Clare? I think you've been given a second chance. If you want to be different from the person you became in the last few years, do it."

"What happens when I get my memory back?"

"Then you've got a choice of who to be, I guess." She nodded to the stove. "Want me to make supper? Or we can order out?"

Clare shook her head. "I'd like to make your favorite meal. I think the ghosts are gone now."

"Oh, good."

The food was terrific, and they both indulged in some cabernet sauvignon to go with it. Cathy told her all about taking fifteen kids to France and had Clare laughing as hard as she'd cried earlier at stories of the kids playing hide-and-seek on the Eiffel Tower, nearly falling into the Seine on the boat tour and mimicking the mimes on the streets of Montmartre. More memories came back, too, the good ones, of her and her sister sitting like this on other couches, sharing their adult lives like sisters should.

Then, as Clare had promised, they put on their pajamas and watched a Lifetime TV show about twins separated at birth. At ten, Cathy yawned.

"You ready for bed?"

"Yeah, the flight tired me out."

"I'm sorry, I should have thought of that earlier."

They said good-night and Clare approached her bedroom with trepidation. She *so* did not want to sleep in that bed. Just seeing it conjured images of her and Brady there in the dream, the chemistry sizzling between them, and the guilt she felt over it. Then she thought of Jonathan. And once again, Clare vowed to be kind to him, to give herself time to discover what they'd had together. Though she was feeling these crazy things for Brady, Clare wasn't going to write off the man she'd been on the verge of moving in with—like the old Clare would have. If she could only remember being close to him, perhaps she'd forestall dreams like she'd had last night.

She saw the lights go out in the office. Another memory came of her and Cathy sleeping in the same bed after their parents died. Grandma let it go on as long as they needed to be together. Feeling foolish, she nonetheless approached her sister's doorway, longing for something, some closeness that she remembered on a visceral level, too.

Cathy's voice came from the bed. "Clare, is something wrong?"

"Um, that's a queen-size bed, you know."

"Yeah, I know."

Now she was embarrassed.

But in the moonlight coming in from the window, she saw Cathy lift up the covers on the other side. Clare rushed to the bed and climbed into it.

"You're still scared, aren't you, at night?"

"Of a lot of things."

"Tell me what else."

"I will. Tomorrow. Go to sleep. I know you're exhausted."

"Good night, Clare."

"Good night."

But Clare didn't fall asleep right away. Not until Cathy reached over and took her hand. Fingers clasped, Clare heard her sister's breathing even out, and then her own eyes closed.

"WELL, IF YOU AREN'T ONE OF the most charming men I've ever met." Cathy smiled over at Jonathan. She was a beautiful, ethereal woman, but Jonathan preferred Clarissa's more vibrant looks. "Flowers and wine." He'd brought them each a different bouquet.

"I'm glad you could come to Rockford, Cathy. Clarissa needs family around."

Family was a hell of a lot better than her friends' constant interference, Jonathan thought. At least Delia Kramer had gone to fetch her son and Mason was on a trip with his daughter. As usual, it was just Langston's threatening presence that Jonathan had to deal with. He thought he and Clarissa were past all this, and then the accident had happened, and she'd forgotten how good they were together. He'd be damned if he wouldn't try to make her remember.

He turned his attention to the present. They were seated at Clarissa's teak dining table, set exquisitely, of course, with fine bone china and sterling. She entered the room smiling as she hadn't smiled at him in weeks, and the grip on his heart eased some. He could tell she was trying harder tonight, and that made him feel better.

"Here she is. Hmm, the food smells good."

"I found the recipe under 'TV station owner's choice.'" She touched his shoulder like she used to.

"There was a lot of fan mail from that one."

"Fan mail?" Cathy asked.

"The show gets a great deal."

"And your being named Rockford's most eligible bachelor helped," Clarissa said.

Cathy looked impressed. "I didn't know that."

"Oh." Clarissa's eyes widened. "Apparently I did."

"I can't tell you how much that means to me."

When they began to eat, he said to Cathy, "Did you know your sister will soon be nationally known?"

He'd already decided he was going to address this. He couldn't do anything about Lillian Langston getting sick, but he could keep mentioning the golden opportunity that loomed over Clarissa's golden head. Cheerfully, he explained the Cooking Channel opportunity to Cathy, but instead of being delighted for her sister, she frowned. He wondered why.

The cheesy chicken and ham was cooked to perfection. Clarissa served it with wild rice and beans, his favorites, too. His wine complemented the meal. After they finished, he stood and nodded to the living room. "Go sit in there and talk, you two. I'm doing KP."

Both women protested.

"No, I'm putting my foot down. I even wore my jeans so I could do this."

Cathy gushed. "Clare, you better hold on to this one. He's a gem."

Jonathan winked. "Keep telling her that."

After he cleaned up, he made decaf coffee and served it with the finger food desserts Clarissa had already set out on a tray. She and Cathy were curled up on a couch in the living room, perusing his photo album. Clarissa glanced at him. "You brought this for me?"

"Yes, I thought it might spark memories." He smiled down at the leather-bound album he'd been keeping for a year. "I hope it's okay."

"More than," Cathy said. She scooted over. "Come sit between us, and tell us about the pictures."

"My pleasure."

The album included his and Clarissa's trips together.

"This is the first time we went to New York. You had a book signing and were thrilled to be asked."

"Did Brady come?" Clarissa wanted to know. "The illustrations are so key to the books."

"No." And he'd made a lot of noise about it. "You were invited because of the popularity of the show."

The pictures covered their summer vacation in Cape Cod, a trip to St. Lucia and a brief excursion to Florida when she was a guest chef on another cooking show. Clarissa leaned into him as the pages progressed: there were photos taken on the set, of her and Jonathan at events around town, some casual ones at his place. She did a double take at his house—his living room, especially. Swallowing hard, she put her hand to her throat.

And he panicked for a moment. There was a memory he didn't want to come back. Not yet, at least. He flipped the page fast.

Cathy commented on how happy she looked, *they* looked, and asked a million questions. More flashes came to Clarissa...

"Oh, I remember that bikini...I never wore it again."

It was skimpy, revealing, and he'd had to coerce her into buying it. "You better not have."

She chuckled at his response, like the old Clarissa.

"Snorkeling? Yes, the fish were so colorful in the Caribbean." They'd had fun that day, and she'd gotten sunburned. He remembered putting the cooling gel on her back.

He longed to tell her they'd made exquisite love in their suite at night, but Cathy was with them, so of course it was inappropriate. But by the time they finished, Jonathan had achieved his goal. Surrounded by so many good memories,

Clarissa stayed close to him, their knees touching. It was as if she'd forgotten their estrangement.

At ten, Cathy went to bed, leaving Clarissa all to Jonathan.

She squeezed his arm where the sleeve of his red shirt was pushed up. "Those are lovely memories, Jonathan. I can see we had fun." She sighed. "This was just what I needed."

"What happened in the pictures isn't the only fun we had, honey."

She stiffened a bit, but didn't pull away. "You mean in bed."

"Uh, huh." He leaned over and brushed his knuckles down her cheek. "Tell me you remember us together like that," he whispered against her lips.

It was subtle, but she inched back. "I wish I could, Jonathan. I'm sure it was nice."

"It was more than nice." He could hear the hurt in his own voice.

"I'm sorry my not remembering our being close hurts you. I just don't know what to do about it." She put her head on his shoulder. They stayed that way for a while, then she yawned.

"Are you tired?" he asked.

"Yes. I still haven't gotten back my stamina. Would you mind going now?"

Yes, he minded. He wanted more, damn it. But he said, "No, of course not." They stood, and he picked up a sweater she'd left on the couch. "Put this on and walk me out."

She donned the sweater and took his outstretched hand. He held it all the way downstairs. When they reached the porch, he pulled her to him without asking for permission. His lips touched hers, gently at first. She went still. When he deepened the kiss, though, he felt her stiffen and pull back. "Jonathan, I—"

She was interrupted by a voice from down below. "Pardon the cliché, but get a room, you two."

Purposely, Jonathan held Clarissa close and smiled. Why not? At the bottom of the steps was Brady Langston, looking as if he wanted to smash somebody's face in.

CHAPTER ELEVEN

BARELY ABLE TO CONTAIN what was seething inside him, Brady stalked up the steps to his condo and, without even changing into workout clothes, headed to the attic to let off some steam. He'd returned home to sleep in his own bed and check on Clare, and found her making out on the porch with Harris. Oh, God, had she slept with the guy while Brady was at his mother's?

He let out an obscenity, then kicked the weight bench. What the hell had he been thinking? Why the hell was he surprised? He should have learned his lesson five weeks ago after…after the biggest mistake of his goddamned life!

He banged the weights around some, then piled as many pounds as he could lift onto the barbell. He was ready to go for the burn when she came into the room. Sensing her presence, he cursed himself for being so attuned to her when she'd let another man grope her minutes ago.

"What's going on up here?" she asked from right behind him. "It sounded like the ceiling was going to cave in."

"Sorry if I disturbed your beauty sleep. You probably need it after…" He let out another curse.

"Excuse me?"

"Never mind. I'll be quieter. Go back to bed." Under his breath he murmured, "*Back* being the operative word."

Nothing. He thought maybe she'd just leave him alone if he ignored her, so he stretched out, lifted the weights from their holder and began the excruciating bench press. But after a few seconds, she appeared in his sight, stared down at him for a moment, then dropped onto the floor. She watched him do ten reps; his muscles were screaming, so he replaced the barbell and sat up.

"What's going on, Brade?"

The green blouse she wore gaped, and at this angle he could see the swell of her breasts. It sent desire shooting through him. Still, he tried not to snap. "I'm bummed. Aftermath of a crisis, I guess. Sammy and Lizzy came to stay with my mother. I thought I'd sleep here tonight, maybe see Cathy."

"She went to bed early."

"How convenient." So much for not snapping. He gritted his teeth, picked up a smaller barbell and began to do arm curls.

Scooting closer, she touched his bare knee. His skin was so sensitized he had to force himself not to moan. "Brady, tell me the truth. What's wrong?"

"I did."

"No, you're angry at me."

"Clare, now isn't a good time to talk about this." He wasn't sure what he would say and do. The images of her with Harris kept flashing through his mind, and instead of depressing him, they were stirring up all kinds of primitive emotions that he didn't want to feel in Clare's presence.

She knelt before him so they were eye level and put both her hands on his knees. His skin prickled at her touch. "I don't care. I want you to tell me what this is all about."

"I…can't." He held her gaze. "You're not ready."

"Brady, please, I've hurt you, and I don't even know why."

His fists curled around the weight. The thought that she didn't remember enraged him. He was a pressure cooker about to erupt. To head off the explosion he stood abruptly, dropped the weight, grabbed her by the shoulders and pulled her up. "Just go, Clare," he gritted out. *"Just go."*

She raised her chin and, damn it, moved in closer. Did she have any idea what she was doing to him? Every muscle in his body leapt at her nearness. "Not until you tell me what this—" she motioned to the room "—and downstairs on the porch was all about."

"You want to know what it's about?" His grip tightened. "It's about this, Clare. It's about *this*."

He yanked her against his chest. His mouth came down hard and he took hers possessively. Without waiting to see if he got a response, he pressed harder, then prodded her lips open with his tongue. He explored her, all but devoured her. Drawing back only to bite her lip, he soothed it with his tongue, then took her mouth again. He was so caught up in what was happening, he didn't realize she was crying until he felt moisture on her jaw when he kissed it. He stopped. "Damn, sweetheart, I'm sorry. Don't—"

"Stop," she said, almost on a hiccup. "Don't stop."

"What?"

"I've been dreaming about this for weeks." She wrapped herself around him. "Please, Brady, don't stop."

At Clare's words, her plea, Brady dragged her to the floor. The rug cushioned her back and his weight on her eclipsed everything, even the lights above. Cast in shadows, all she could see were his taut features. But it felt right to have his bare legs tangle with hers, his chest crush into her, his mouth ravage hers. Just like in the dream.

"Clare, oh, man, Clare." His absorption in her spurred her desire—every muscle, every nerve in her body responded. Had anyone ever loved her like this?

Yes, someone had, once.

But her mind got muddled when he ripped open her shirt and sent her buttons flying. The clasp on her leopard print bra snapped, and her breasts spilled into his hands. She gasped as he took a nipple in his mouth. His hand trailed down her rib cage to her shorts; he yanked open the zipper, and cupped her. Rubbed.

"Brady, yes, yes, Brady…" She exploded into a burst of color and light and feelings so intense she started to cry again. Steeped in the mind-numbing pleasure, all she could say was, "Yes, yes, yes."

When she came back to reality, Brady was braced over her, his forearms on either side of her head. His face was a mask of pain. "Oh, baby, I'm…"

Intuitively she knew he was going to apologize, which was the last thing she wanted. "Next."

"What?"

"You're next."

She could tell she surprised him by pushing on his chest, unbalancing him, and climbing on top of him before he could say more. After she straddled him, she yanked his T-shirt over his head, revealing dark springy hair. She kissed her way across it, around his pecs. Not only did she remember his scent but also his texture, and the contour of his muscles. Something niggled at her, something about the familiarity of his body, a déjà vu of some kind, but she was distracted by her own movements. She left no part of his torso untouched—his abs, his ribs, his waist. She made quick work of his belt and his zipper. When she freed him of the clothes, she took his penis in her hands and massaged him.

With the last, Brady jackknifed up and grabbed her shoulders, the reaction unconscious, spontaneous. "That feels good." He held her so tight he knew he'd leave bruises, but he'd lost control. "Cla-re," he gasped as she scooted lower, bent over and touched the tip of him with her mouth.

He flipped her fast and dragged off her shorts and her leopard bikinis. He tore at the rest of his clothes, too, and with one last burst of sanity, he fumbled for a condom in his wallet and sheathed himself. She stretched out before him, opened to him and he plunged inside her.

Nothing, *nothing* had ever felt so right. He pushed hard, uncontrollably. She spiraled again and he waited until she peaked, filling her with thrust after thrust after thrust. Then he came in one blinding flash.

Brady knew the instant that awareness dawned for her. He was still inside her, staring down into her face, which was the most beautiful sight he'd ever seen. There was recognition in those eyes, too. She just watched him a minute. Then she whispered, "We did this before."

He nodded, his heart beating faster than when he'd orgasmed. Thinking how cruel it was to have her like this again, only for her to remember exactly what would take her away from him, he waited.

"The night of the accident. We made love. I remember it, but not much else."

"I'll tell you all of it."

Suddenly she grabbed his shoulders. "Not yet. Stay with me a little longer."

Thankful for the reprieve, he rolled them to their sides and held her close. When she shivered, he reached for a yoga blanket she'd left on the floor a lifetime ago and covered them. She seemed content to let him stroke her bare arm, occasionally kiss her hair.

A good ten minutes passed before she said, "All right. Tell me what happened."

"Just that night?"

"No, what led up to it." Her hair brushed his chest as she shook her head. "You said we were friends. And then we grew apart."

"We were friends, for a while. When I moved here, my father had recently died so I was in no shape for a relationship, but I needed friends. And for a long time, I was strung out from my divorce. You were dating casually, then I did. But we really liked each other, Clare, connected over the losses we'd experienced. And we had similar outlooks on life. Our personalities just clicked. We were soul mates. When we began to work together on the books, I started having different kinds of feelings for you, but I didn't want things to change because they were going so great for us. Eventually, though, I fell in love with you."

She buried her nose in his chest. "Oh, Brady. Did you tell me? I can't believe I'd forget that."

"No, I didn't. I let it go for a year, afraid I'd upset the balance of all our lives. And I knew you didn't feel the same."

"How could you know?"

"I just could."

She snorted, of all things. "Anna said she thinks I've been attracted to you...like this...for a long time."

"Why would you be talking to Anna about that?"

"Um, I've been having dreams about you, Brady. Sexual dreams."

"Oh, man, that's great. Tell me about them."

"Finish your story first. Why didn't you do anything, say anything, when your feelings changed?"

"Harris beat me to the punch. He came into your life like a whirlwind and swept you away from me. Away from Delia and Max, too."

"*That* I know because everybody's told me. I can't express how bad I feel for abandoning all of you."

"We all grew apart, especially me and you. I was jealous as hell but didn't know what to do. When you started sleeping with him, I thought I'd die."

"Oh, Brady, I'm so sorry." He didn't say anything. "What happened to bring us to making love?"

His grip on her tightened. "I told you before that he was close to talking you into moving out. He wanted you away from us. I panicked. The night of the accident I got you alone and we did argue, like I said. But I also confessed that I loved you. That I'd loved you for a long time."

Clare gasped. "I remember…"

"WHY ARE YOU BRINGING me up here?" she asked when he dragged her to their attic. "Jonathan's expecting me at his place, and I'm already late."

"I know. I have to tell you something."

She saw the pain in his face and calmed down. "I know things have been strained between us lately. I'm sorry about that. And that you're angry about my moving out."

"Try devastated."

"Really?" She moved in close to hug him. "I—"

He thrust her away. "No, don't. Don't apologize, and don't touch me."

"Why?"

"You really don't know, do you?"

She shook her head.

He looked to the ceiling. "How humbling."

"What, Brady? Tell me."

"I love you, damn it! I have for a long time. And not as a friend."

"*What?*"

He watched her. Finally, he came toward her, said, "What the hell?" and kissed her.

SHE'D LET HIM, FOUND herself kissing him back.

And they'd made love like they had just minutes ago…

Clare had to make a conscious effort to breathe. At last, she was able to talk. "I was a willing participant, Brady. I remember now."

He drew in a deep breath, too, and kissed her forehead. "Yeah, you were." A sad chuckle. "Twice."

"What happened afterward?"

"Sanity returned. You started to feel guilty about Harris."

"I was in a committed relationship, and I cheated on him."

"I know." The words were wrenched from him. "You got up and moved away. Covered yourself, which drove me crazy. You asked me why I seduced you when I knew you were with Jonathan. I got angry and said it took two."

"It does. I don't know why I said that."

"Guilt is my guess. We started yelling at each other, and the last thing you said was that making love with me was a mistake."

"That must have hurt."

"It just about killed me. You left angry and upset. So angry and upset, Clare, that you were out on the road alone and had the accident." He drew in a heavy breath. "Making love with me caused your amnesia."

"Usually amnesia's caused by something bad, something traumatic."

"Maybe it was traumatic for you to make love with one man and be in a serious relationship with another."

"Forgetting my entire past out of guilt for making love with you seems extreme to me. Especially if I wanted it as much as you did."

"Then maybe yours isn't a case of psychological amnesia and was caused by the blow to your head."

"Maybe." She thought for a second. "What time did this happen?"

"We came up here about ten. You left around midnight."

"Two hours before the accident?" She sat up now. "Where was I all that time?"

"I don't know."

Clare tried hard to visualize the series of events that night. Maybe she *was* working out her guilt on that road and had the accident. Or maybe… "Maybe I went to Jonathan's."

"I thought that at first. But, Clare, as much as I dislike the guy, he does love you and he would have come forward with that information in order to help you remember."

"You didn't."

"Yeah, but I had reason to keep it from you. At first I didn't want to push you too much, like the doctors warned us not to do. Then I couldn't stand keeping the argument a secret, so I confessed on movie night. I guess I couldn't bear to bring up the rest."

"I can understand that."

"In any case, we need to find out if you went to Harris's house after you and I made love."

"I can't ask him. What if he doesn't know about us?"

She shivered, and he tucked the blanket around her nakedness. "He probably *doesn't* know, given the way he's been trying to rush our physical relationship."

Brady grabbed her hand. "He's rushing you?"

"Yes, I wasn't ready for that kiss you witnessed."

He looked around at their clothes and makeshift bed and his face lightened. "You were ready for this."

"I was. The chemistry between us has been driving me crazy. Maybe it was the same the last time. I do remember wanting to make love to you that night when it happened."

"I'm glad for that, but I still think I caused your accident." He shook his head. "I'm not proud of myself for seducing you."

"Brady, you clearly didn't seduce me this time." She watched him carefully. "Which leads me to believe you didn't seduce me last time, either."

"No?"

"Nope. But I do feel guilty about both. I could barely let Jonathan kiss me, but I wanted to be with you tonight. A lot."

"What does all this mean, Clare? For us?"

"I don't know. I wish I could remember what happened the rest of the night after the accident."

Gently, Brady smoothed down her hair. "One thing *I* know is the situation's definitely changed. You can't go running back to Harris after telling me how you feel about me."

"I won't. But I can't simply cut him out of my life, either."

"Not the answer I want, babe."

"I'm sorry. It's the best I can do."

"I won't let this happen all over again, Clare. He can't have you again." She could see the pain behind the autocratic comment.

"I'm making my own decisions now, Brady. I have to.

But I will explain this one to you. I feel terrible about abandoning you and Delia and Max. Even my own sister. I'm putting that behind me."

"That's good, sweetheart."

"Don't you see? That means I can't just abandon Jonathan, either. The old me would have, but I won't do it now. I'm done treating people that way."

He just stared at her.

"Please try to understand, Brade. I need to figure all this out in my own time."

Like she knew he would, like he'd always done, he nodded, putting her own welfare above his own. "All right."

"Thank you."

He grabbed her arms and yanked her close. "Just remember what you have with me. Remember this." His mouth closed over hers in a hard and possessive kiss.

She was dizzy when she pulled back but managed a little smile. "Don't worry, I'll never forget that."

CHAPTER TWELVE

"CLARE, WHAT are you doing up so early?" Cathy spoke the words from the doorway to the kitchen where she stood, wearing a pretty green robe.

Shaky today from lack of sleep, and because she'd had time to internalize what she'd done last night, Clare glanced at the clock. 7:00 a.m. "I'm sorry, did I wake you?"

"No, I was awake. I heard you come in late, though. Did you go home with Jonathan for a while?"

Clare groaned. "No." She took the scrubbed carrots and began slicing them with a large knife. "I...um, saw Brady." Boy, did she see Brady—his beautiful chest, impressive abs...impressive everything! She couldn't stop thinking about him, though today she was feeling even more guilt because of Jonathan. Was that what happened the last time—the juxtaposition of two conflicting emotions that led to her amnesia?

Cathy came farther into the kitchen and poured herself coffee. From over by the pot, she asked, "Isn't Brady staying at his mom's anymore?"

"Yes, he is. But his sister went over there last night, so he came home to sleep."

"How is he? I know you've been worried about him."

He's wonderful. Fantastic. A very skilled lover. "He

seems better about his mom." She put the carrots in a large Ziploc bag and started chopping the celery. "He's heading back over there today."

Circling around to the other side of the counter, Cathy sat on a stool and watched her. "I was hoping to see him."

Clare didn't say anything.

"All right. You're doing what you always did...chopping up a storm because you're upset. Who caused it, Brady or Jonathan?"

"Neither." Clare had to clear her throat at the lie. "I'm doing that food demo at the nursing home, remember? You're coming with me. Then we have to go to Lillian's house to work on the recipes." She chopped harder. "I promised. I have to go. I wouldn't if—"

Cathy reached across the counter, stayed her hand and took the knife.

"Why did you do that?"

"I'm saving your fingers. You have no idea what you're doing."

Clare stared at her sister, then began to laugh...a nervous, hysterical laugh. "Oh, God, *you* have no idea how true that is."

Standing, Cathy got Clare a cup of coffee then dragged her by the arm to the table. "Sit and tell me what happened."

Clare dropped down into the chair because she couldn't find the will to protest. And besides, she remembered that she used to confide in Cathy in the past. "We made love last night."

"Usually that's cause for celebration. Was it odd because you don't remember Jonathan?"

"Oh, good Lord." Clare shook her head, finally faced her sister. "Not me and Jonathan. Me and Brady."

Coffee sloshed over Cathy's cup onto the table. She was openmouthed, too. "I...what...holy cow!"

"I know." Clare buried her face in her hands. "I'm still in shock."

"Was it?"

"Was it what?"

"A shock to your system?"

Clare stilled. All night she'd tried not to let this in, but it was bubbling up inside her and ready to spill over. "No. It felt right."

A brow raised, Cathy just watched her.

"What?" asked Clare.

"The body doesn't lie. It knows what it wants. Where it belongs."

Closing her eyes, Clare shook her head. "How can this be good? I was in a committed relationship with Jonathan—for God's sake, we were moving in together—and I cheated on him. I feel terrible."

"You don't remember any of that, sweetie. You acted on how you feel now, today. From what I can see, there's no guilt to be had in that."

Clare looked at Cathy. "There's more."

Her sister waited.

"It wasn't the first time. I remembered the night of the accident. Brady and I made love then, too." And it was just as fantastic. "I got upset after, told him it was a mistake and left the house."

"Where did you go?"

"I don't know. I don't remember anything after leaving Brady. I'm not sure what I did before the accident."

"If you'd gone to Jonathan's, wouldn't he have told you?"

"I don't know that he would have. Or should have.

The therapists said not to rush the memories. And Brady didn't tell me we made love, for some of the same reasons, at least."

Frowning, Cathy toyed with the napkin. "I suppose so. But Brady did tell you about the argument you two had and his part in your accident, on movie night. Shouldn't Jonathan have at least told you that you went there? It's been over a month since the accident." She scowled.

"What are you thinking?"

"Maybe Jonathan doesn't want you to remember what happened, Clare."

"Why wouldn't he?"

"Maybe if you told him about Brady and then you got amnesia, he saw it as a second chance. He could be hoping you'd never remember what you did with Brady."

"Cathy, that night, I told Brady it was a mistake. If I went to see Jonathan, then I would have told him that, too."

"Maybe."

"No, Jonathan would never dupe me like that all these weeks. He cares too much about me."

"Well, I agree with that. He's a nice guy, and it's obvious he loves you."

"I must have felt the same about him. If I could just remember..." Her heart clenched so tight in her chest she put her hand over it. "But you're right about one thing. Brady told me he loved me that night. And I totally freaked."

"Clare, he's loved you forever."

"He said that, too." She patted her chest with her palm. "Am I the only one who didn't know it?"

"Probably. I brought it up a few times, but by then you were with Jonathan and I stopped mentioning it."

"Why can't I remember the rest?"

"I don't know." A pause while Cathy sipped her coffee. "What are you going to do?"

"Right now, I'm going to finish getting the food ready for the demo. Then I'm going to cook lunch for twenty senior citizens."

"You'll have to see Brady, too. Like you said, we're supposed to go over to Lillian's."

"With you as a buffer."

"Clare, Brady's not the enemy. And for a long time he was your best friend. Don't worry about seeing him. He's always taken care of you."

"He was hurt last night because I wouldn't end my relationship with Jonathan. People in pain don't necessarily take care of those they love."

"Still, I have faith in him."

Clare threw back her chair. "I can't stand rehashing this. Let's finish up here."

With Cathy's help, Clare prepared the rest of the food and then they showered, dressed—coincidentally both in red—and arrived at Serene Gardens by ten. When she walked in, she remembered the place clearly. What it looked like. What it smelled like. Who would be there.

Twenty people were seated in the rows of chairs set up in front of the open kitchen area, which was at the end of the dining room. The residents were short and tall, white-haired, some in wheelchairs or using walkers.

"There she is," an older gentleman spoke out. He rose and hobbled over to her. "Clare dear. How nice to see you."

"Mr. Antonelli. Hello."

Cathy's eyes bulged. Clare smiled.

She remembered Mrs. Thompson, Mr. Clark, Mrs. Agnew. And many others who greeted her.

A tiny woman made her way over in a walker. "Hello, young lady."

"Oh." Well, it was too good to be true. "I'm sorry, I don't remember you."

"How could you? We've never met. I just moved into this place."

After Clare greeted the residents, the manager—Deb Sykes, whom she also recognized—came in and drew Clare away from the others. Cathy had been setting up for the demo on the counter. It was time to begin. Clare was glad, because it would take her mind off everything. Cooking always did.

Just as she faced the crowd from behind the open counter, Jonathan walked in. So much for forgetting. He looked happy—he didn't know what she'd done after he left last night. Dressed in a nice suit, he was perfectly groomed. She gave a little wave, he smiled genuinely, then she said to the group, "Hello, everyone. It's good to be back."

They clapped. Oh, how sweet. Clare had experienced so much fear and anxiety since she'd woken up in the hospital with no memory that she luxuriated in the warm, fuzzy feeling that filled her at their acceptance. She also wondered how she'd ever let this relationship with the nursing home go.

"First I'd like to introduce my sister, Cathy, who's my sous-chef."

Smiling out at the group, Cathy waved. "Hi, there."

"Today, we're going to be making turkey noodle soup, and then I'm going to prepare lasagna. You can have the soup now, for lunch, and the lasagna for dinner. How does that sound?"

They cheered like little kids.

"Like the Cooking Channel."

"Like old times."

"We missed you, girl."

Cathy had a ball at the demo and wanted to stay for lunch. They weren't due at Lillian's house until two, so Clare agreed. Before she could take a seat, Jonathan came up to her.

"Hello, Clarissa." He kissed her cheek and studied her face. "You all right? You look tired."

"I had a hard time sleeping."

He seemed surprised. "I hope I didn't have anything to do with that."

"No, you didn't. Do you want to sit with Cathy and me?"

His grin was self-effacing. "I think Mrs. DeBellis would be insulted if I did that."

She'd forgotten about the small woman who had a big crush on Jonathan. He'd come to the nursing home, too, to keep her company while she cooked for the older people.

As he crossed the room, Clare saw Mrs. DeBellis's face light with pleasure. When Jonathan kissed her cheek and sat down, she beamed. He was a nice man, generous with his time and money. And thinking about that made Clare's good mood fizzle out like a candle in the rain. She was an unfaithful girlfriend, a cheater, and she didn't deserve Jonathan's love and commitment.

Because every time she saw him, she realized her heart belonged to Brady.

"WHAT'S WRONG, SON?" Brady's mother asked the question from the kitchen table where she'd come out to sit for lunch. The doctor had said she should be up and about and they'd just finished Clare's minestrone soup.

At the sink where he was filling the dishwasher, he mumbled, "Nothing, why?"

"You're lying. You look like you lost your best friend...again."

"Maybe I did." He came back to the table and scrubbed his hand over his face. He hadn't shaved, and his beard was scratchy. He could barely shower, he was so bummed. And confused. And, all right, angry. How could she make love to him as she had last night, with her body *and* her soul, then say she didn't know what she was going to do about Harris? It was almost as bad as the last time when she declared what they'd done together was a mistake!

Okay, sure, she said she wasn't going to abandon anyone anymore in her life. He wanted her back to the old Clare who wouldn't have done that, but did she have to start with Harris?

His mom grasped his hand. "Is it something more than what you told me the night Sammy bumped into Clare at the restaurant?"

Brady had only confessed to his mother that he was responsible for Clare's accident, that they'd had a fight and she'd left the house angry. He didn't tell her they'd made love, nor would he share that information today. Briefly, he wondered if he was too ashamed to reveal what he'd done, or if he was just protecting Clare's privacy.

"Honey, you can tell me anything."

"I know, Mom. I just can't talk about this."

"Hello!" Clare's voice from the front of the house. Just the sound of it made his gut clench as images from last night flooded him.

Please, Brady, make love to me... Yes, Brady, yes.

"Come on in, dear," Lillian called out. "We're in the kitchen."

They heard the screen door open and close. Brady had wanted to turn on the air-conditioning he'd had put in last year because it was warm today, but his mother hadn't liked it on since she came home from the hospital. He was hot, and got even hotter when Clare came to the kitchen entrance.

She was dressed in red polka dots, but the color washed her out, and she looked exhausted. Her hair was fluffy around her cheeks, and her face was drawn. Damn, he'd hurt her again. It doused his anger immediately.

"Hi, there." She smiled at his mother, but it didn't reach her eyes. "I brought Cathy with me."

Cathy stepped up to her side. "Hi, Brady. Lillian."

Brady stood and crossed to Cathy. Clare still wouldn't look at him. He hugged her sister, and when Cathy went to greet his mom, Brady stepped in front of Clare. Gently, he placed his hands on her arms and felt her trembling. "Easy, now. It's okay." He pulled her close. "Everything's going to be all right."

"I'm a wreck," she whispered against his chest.

"Me, too. Let's make a pact. We'll try to relax around each other." Because he knew it would help her, he added, "I don't want to upset Mom."

"Of course not." Still, she clung to him. Took a deep breath and let it out. He kissed her hair.

"Better, now?"

She nodded. He stepped back, took her hand and led her to the table.

Cathy gave their joined hands a glance, then said, "I hope it's all right that I came. I love being part of Clare's life again."

"Of course it is." Brady grinned. "We have to catch up, too."

Clare sat down, but Brady didn't. She said, "So, we have two more recipes to pick out and, what, four more stories to record?"

"Uh-huh." His mom looked better than she had since she'd come home, and Clare's arrival had perked her up even more. "I had some new ideas I wanted to run by you, dear, if that's all right."

Brady picked up his sketch pad, which sat on the kitchen table. "I'm going outside to work on the drawings. It's too warm in here for me and, besides, I'll be distracted by the chatter."

All three women looked at him. His mother smiled, Cathy seemed concerned and Clare bewildered. Getting out of her sight was the least he could do for her. He squeezed her shoulder before he left.

There was a big hammock in the backyard that was one of his favorite places. He'd always come out here when he was conflicted, and a lot of times his dad had joined him, sat in a nearby chair and they'd talked. Would his dad be ashamed of what Brady had done with Clare? Or would he understand his son's driving need for the woman?

Damn it. If only she hadn't felt so good under his hands. Hadn't clung to him as if she'd never let go.

But she had let go. Twice.

Situating himself in a position where he had room to draw, he studied the recipes that Clare and his mother had chosen, which he'd stuck in a pocket of the pad. He'd decided to put a member of his family in each sketch. He started with the pudding paint. That had been a hoot. He could still see himself slathering the pudding in the girls' hair. Their readers would appreciate that story. He began to sketch Sam's and Jules's curls with gobs of pudding dripping from them—along with just his hands. The preliminary drawing made him laugh out loud.

"That's good to hear." Brady looked up to see Cathy standing by him. Engrossed in his work, he had no idea how much time had passed. "I know I'm interrupting, and I won't stay long, but I wanted a minute alone with you."

"It's so good to see you, Cath. Of course, sit."

She dropped down into one of the big wooden Adirondack chairs they'd painted forest-green.

"How was France?"

"Don't ask. Chaperoning fifteen teenagers in the most romantic city in the world was not pretty."

Again he laughed.

"How are you doing?"

He made a show of closing the pad and setting it and his pencil on his lap. "Great."

Her smile gentle, she shook her head. "You're not. You're as upset as she is."

"What do you mean?"

"She told me about last night."

He didn't expect this. "She did?"

"Brady, what's going on with you two?"

"How much did she tell you?"

Cathy related what Clare had said.

"You know as much as I do. She feels like she betrayed Harris. For the second time. But she cares about me. And she's bound and determined not to revert to her old ways of just abandoning people. That includes Harris, now."

Her sister frowned. "Something doesn't add up."

"What do you mean?"

"For one thing, where was she for two hours that night after she left you?"

His stomach cramped as the nightmare of where she might have gone formed in his brain. He'd kept it at bay since Clare's coma, but after last night, and here in her sister's presence, it forced its way out of his unconscious mind. He just stared at Cathy.

"Do you think she went over to Jonathan's house?"

"Uh-huh. And I'm afraid of what she did there."

For a minute, Cathy looked puzzled. Then her eyes widened. "No, Brady, Clare wouldn't make love with two men in one night."

"He might have insisted." Brady swallowed back the bile that rose in his throat at the thought. "If she told him what happened between us, and that she regretted it, he could have…asked her to prove her remorse was true." Brady could barely utter the words, barely let in the ugly possibility. "I've seen my share of Lifetime television where something similar happens, Cath."

"But Clare's psyche—how could she handle that?"

He scowled. "Maybe she couldn't. Maybe that's what she doesn't remember, because it was too much for her to take in."

"Oh, God, poor Clare, if that's true."

"It's my fault." He rolled his eyes. "And then I did it again."

"Brady, this is supposition, and I'm not sure I buy it all." Cathy ignored his guilt comment. "Why wouldn't Jonathan come forward with what he knows, then? Say she was there before the accident?"

"If that's the kind of thing you were keeping secret," Brady said hoarsely, "would you confess to it?"

"I don't know. I'd at least say she was there."

"He probably doesn't want her to remember."

Sighing heavily, Cathy rubbed the arm of the chair.

Brady asked, "Do you think she'll talk to him about that night, now that she remembers what happened between us?"

"She doesn't know what she's going to do."

Clare appeared on the back patio with her phone at her ear. Brady watched her as she frowned, listened, talked. When she clicked off, she glanced over at him and Cathy, then walked toward them. Her shoulders sagged, and the expression in her eyes was bleak.

"What now?" Brady asked when Clare reached him.

"That was Jonathan. He's rescheduled with the Cooking Channel. He wants to go to New York on Friday, have the meeting late in the afternoon and stay for the weekend. I said I couldn't because Cathy's only here until Monday, but I have to go down for an overnight."

"An overnight?" Brady said. The thought unpalatable.

Cathy stood. "I'm going to go keep Lillian company. You two should talk." She headed to the house.

Clare dropped down into the chair. Brady watched her.

"Did you get any sleep last night?" she asked.

"Not much. You?"

"Mostly, I prowled around the house. I think I caught a couple of hours."

"You didn't go see him after you left me?"

"No! Of course not."

He cocked his head. "Why is that thought so repugnant to you?"

"It just is, after what we did together."

"Cathy and I were talking. She agrees that maybe you went to Jonathan's house in the missing two hours that night."

"I told you before, he'd have said something if I had."

"You were feeling pretty guilty about what we did."

"I do today, too."

He looked away. "I see."

"No, don't be upset. I'm feeling guilty because I can't stop thinking about last night. I can't stop remembering what it was like with you the last time, too. Those details are all there. In living color."

"Then, damn it, leave Harris for me."

She shook her head. "I told you last night why I can't do that right now. I'm done abandoning people. I just can't walk away from him until I remember everything."

His fists curled. "What you can't do is tell me what you just did—that you're thinking about me, us together—then say you're going away with another guy."

"I'm going to New York, Brady. You know how much I want that show on the Cooking Channel. I want to pursue it, and if I cancel again, like I did with your mom's situation, I won't get another shot at it."

Because he wanted what was best for her, he didn't try to refute her words. "You're right. I know that. But I hate you being there with him overnight."

Sliding to the edge of the chair, she took his hand. Hers was trembling a bit, making him feel like scum. He grasped it tightly. "I *do* know one thing, Brade. I won't be staying in the same room with him."

"Did you tell him that?"

"Yes."

"How'd he take it?"

"Badly. But I won't stay in the same room with him, and I won't sleep with him. I don't want to. Not after us." She ran her free hand through her hair. "Just the thought of making love with two men within a few days is untenable. I couldn't live with myself if I did."

She meant the statement to be comforting, but it wasn't.

Because Brady remembered Cathy's words, which exacerbated his deeply buried fears.

Clare wouldn't make love with two men in one night... her psyche...how could she live with that?

THE REST OF THE WEEK PASSED in a blur. Clare finished choosing the recipes with Lillian and determining the family stories to go with them. Brady stayed over at his mom's to work on the drawings. Clare knew he was being considerate of her feelings, and with him not around, she *could* think more clearly.

She and Cathy had had a wonderful few days, playing tennis, making fancy meals, looking through photo albums. Early memories flooded back as if a dam had been broken when she slept with Brady; now she recalled almost everything. She remembered most of her childhood, and when they came across pictures of their parents, and her mom and dad formed fully in her mind, once again Clare cried as if she'd just lost them. Friends, cousins, school—everything was just there!

She'd told Jonathan she was busy with Cathy, but she'd had to see him yesterday to prepare a strategy for the upcoming interview. The meeting hadn't gone well.

"I DON'T UNDERSTAND WHY you can't stay in New York for the weekend. The Cooking Channel people offered us tickets to any play we want to see."

"Jonathan, Cathy's going back Monday. I can't leave her alone for the whole weekend. Look, get tickets for Friday night. I agreed to stay until Saturday."

He became angry, which precipitated the next statement. "I'm reserving one room for us."

It was then that her temper spiked. "We already discussed this! I said I'm not ready for that, and I resent you pressuring me about it."

"You need to help your memory along, Clarissa. Remember the pictures I brought. It can be like that again."

"No. I won't stay in the same room with you. And don't keep bringing it up. I mean it."

He was upset by that, but this time, instead of feeling guilty, Clare got even angrier. "Don't push me, Jonathan…"

THE DOORBELL RANG. Cathy was having lunch with some of her old high-school friends, so Clare left her office to answer the door. She hoped it wasn't Jonathan.

It wasn't. It was the best thing in the world. "Donny!"

"Aunt Clare!" The little boy jumped into her arms. "I knew you'd remember me."

"I do." She hugged him close. She knew everything about him—his little-boy scent, the feel of his skinny body, even the texture of his red hair. And events: being his godmother, standing for the bus with Delia when he went to kindergarten, Christmases and Halloweens and overnights with just him and her.

"You can come out, Mom."

Delia appeared in the doorway. There were tears in her eyes.

But mischief danced in the boy's. "I wanted to see if you'd know who I was without her."

She dragged Donny inside, and Delia followed. Clare's heart, which had been heavy for weeks, and the past few days especially, lightened so much, she felt like a different person.

"Can we make cookies?" Donny asked.

"Of course. I got this great recipe for elephant ears."

"Cool."

"Donny, let Aunt Clare catch her breath."

"I don't want to." Clare laughed as she took his hand and led him to the kitchen. "I want to spend time with my favorite man."

"Uncle Brady's your favorite man," he said innocently.

Clare winced. "He's one of them."

"He's my favorite. Since I don't have a dad." He looked to Delia. "Sorry. I had a dad, but he died."

Clare ruffled his hair. "I know what you meant, honey."

"Uncle Brady says he can be my… What, Mom?"

"Your surrogate father."

"It means to act like my dad. He takes me to lots of things."

Vividly, Clare could recall Brady picking up Donny for father-son scout banquets, taking the boy trick-or-treating, and going to open house at school with Delia. As in the past, when he did these things, she felt so much pride and admiration for him and the kind of person he was.

"I know he does. And he loves you as much as your father would have."

In the kitchen, Donny dragged a stool to the other side of the counter, just as he had countless times, while Clare got out Lillian's recipe and the ingredients. Automatically, she handed him the measuring cups.

"Why are the cookies called elephant ears?" Donny asked as he carefully scooped out flour.

"Wait till you see them. Their shape and the cinnamon lines swirling through them make them look like the ears of elephants."

As always, he went right on to the next topic. "Mom says you don't remember anything, but you do."

"It's all coming back," Clare told him.

From across the counter, Delia smiled. "Really, all of it?"

"Well, the night of the accident is still fuzzy." Except for making love with Brady. "But I'm remembering mostly everything else."

As she looked at her friend, she had a flash of Delia crying over an argument they'd had. *How can you be so callous?*

A flash of Delia yelling. *You've obviously made your choices, Clare. I might put up with this, but I won't let Donny suffer. You're to stay out of his life when he gets back from his grandparents.*

That had happened when Clare had told everybody she was considering moving out. Max had been furious, but Brady's reaction had been the worst. Brady had been crushed.

"Aunt Clare, you okay?"

"Dee, I'm sorry. I'm so sorry."

"You remember?"

"Yes, how could I..."

There was a loud knock on the door. Another interruption. "Hello. Anybody home?"

"In here, Uncle Brady." Donny scampered off the stool and when Brady came to the doorway, the boy flung himself at the man. "I missed you."

Brady hiked him up and held him close. He savored Donny's hug. "Oh, man, I missed you, too." Clare melted at the sight of their reunion.

Donny got down and pulled Brady to the stool next to his mother. "Sit with Mom while me and Aunt Clare bake. Like you used to."

Brady sat and looked over at Clare. "Yeah," he said, "Like old times."

"Aunt Clare remembers me. She remembers everything."

His face clouded. "Everything?"

Delia nodded. "About us."

Clare was struggling to keep it together. The emotion of seeing Donny, what she had just remembered about Delia, especially, and the memory of how badly she'd behaved were all battering at her.

As if he sensed it, Brady got up and poured himself some coffee. Then he crossed to the side of the counter where Clare was, slid his arm around her, and pulled her close. He didn't say anything for a second, then looked down. "Oh, man, you're gonna love elephant ears, kid."

Grateful for his silent support, Clare just leaned into him.

CHAPTER THIRTEEN

CLARE RECOGNIZED New York City as soon as she stepped out of the cab in front of the Marriott Marquis Hotel. The blinking lights of Times Square, the cacophony—horns blowing, the chatter of throngs of people on the street—were familiar to her. Not on a visceral level. But on an "I've been here" level. She'd stood in this exact spot before, marveling at the multistory hotel with its skyscraper-height, high-speed glassed-in elevators and the red sign. Clare knew she'd had lunch at the pizza place across the way. Oh, God, with Grandma Boneli, who'd always wanted to visit the Big Apple. Clare and Cathy had brought her here. Clare had gone to Broadway shows with Jonathan like revivals of *A Chorus Line* and *Spring Awakening*. Brady had favored *Seussical, The Lion King* and *Avenue Q,* of course. It was so good to remember details.

"Clarissa, are you all right?" Next to her, Jonathan grasped her arm, his voice solicitous. His pique at her had not diminished, but he'd been civil since picking her up today. She'd been equally polite.

"Yes, of course."

"Too much?" There was tenderness in his tone. She'd always loved it when he talked to her that way, but today it made her seriously uncomfortable, and she had to force herself not to inch away.

"No, it's helpful that I'm remembering."

Guilt coiled in her stomach. Clare hadn't revealed to Jonathan how much of her memory had returned this week because she might just have to tell him why—making love with Brady—and she wasn't ready to do that.

"We should check in. Here, let me get your bag."

"No, I'm fine. It rolls."

With her memory's return came a good deal of self-confidence and her characteristic independence. In some ways, she'd forgotten her real personality. And definitely, she'd been vulnerable and fragile for too long. *That* person simply wasn't her.

She also remembered her personal preferences. She liked the clothes she was wearing today—the expensive silk, nice jewelry and designer shoes. Yet she felt comfortable in jeans and casual outfits, too. Not for the first time, she wondered if it was possible to meld the old and new Clare. Who would that person be? If she hadn't had to take this trip, she would have gotten in to see Anna Summers to talk again, now that she pretty much remembered everything.

"Our appointment is at four. We've got plenty of time to check in and have a light lunch, since we're doing dinner early, before the theater."

"Fine."

As they walked into the hotel, tension sizzled between them at what wasn't being voiced—that she wouldn't stay in the same room with him. And she was angry right back that he expected her to sleep with him, if he thought she remembered nothing! As a matter of fact, she did remember their sex life, but she had only vague images of it compared to the Technicolor memory of her and Brady.

Once again, Clare realized that she'd thought for a long time she and Jonathan were perfectly suited, with the same tastes, the same goals, the same outlook on life. But she didn't *feel* the same about all these things now that her closeness with Brady had come front and center.

The bellman on the ground level relieved them of their baggage, and she and Jonathan took the elevator to the eighth floor. He approached the registration desk and, after a speedy check-in, came back to her.

"We're all set. Adjoining rooms, if that's all right," he said tightly.

"Yes, of course."

"I didn't know if it would be."

"Please, don't be surly about this."

His eyes were grim, and Clare saw his insecurity and his worry. He was afraid of losing her. It made her feel bad, because basically Jonathan was a good man. He'd showed it to her many times. The conflicting emotions she was experiencing were overwhelming.

As if to confirm her thoughts, he said, "I won't be difficult. I want this television show for you, Clarissa. I want you to be happy."

They took an hour to settle into their rooms and dress. She put away what few clothes she'd brought, donned a professional two-piece mauve suit and freshened her makeup.

Odd, how the sophisticated woman staring back at her was familiar now. She *did* know she'd had longer hair. She *did* know she usually wore a considerable amount of makeup, but she'd been eschewing it since the accident for some simple blush and lipstick.

Because the woman peering back at her also remembered the Clare of ponytails and beer, of racing with Brady on one of their runs, of caring about him, Delia, Donny and Max as if they were her family.

And more, of course. With Brady. As she sat before the mirror she imagined him, standing behind her, leaning over, kissing her neck, sliding his hand inside her jacket, touching her intimately.

The knock on the adjoining door brought her out of not a real memory, but a fantasy. That intimacy had never happened, but since she'd slept with him, she found herself thinking about him like this all the time. "Damn," she murmured. Then, aloud, "Coming."

Jonathan was more amiable as they took the glass elevator down, giving them a spectacular view of the hotel in all its splendid glory. She'd always appreciated the open seating area, the huge potted plants, gilt trim everywhere.

"I made reservations at La Grande for lunch."

"Sounds good."

"It's your favorite restaurant here."

"Hmm."

He watched her. "I hate this strain between us."

She hated the sadness in his voice. Clare wanted to reach over and take his hand. That would be the natural thing to do. But she found herself unable to make the gesture. "Me, too."

"Can we table it, for now? We always had so much fun in the city."

"I'd like that."

At his mention of fun in the city, another memory came full blown. She'd had fun here before she met Jonathan with Dee, Max and Brady, all of them exploring the Village with relish. She and Brady had once taken the literary tour there, to all the famous places well-known authors had lived and frequented.

Still, she'd made a conscious decision to come to New York with Jonathan, and to wait for her full memory to come back before she made further choices about her life, so she tried to show him she was enjoying herself.

And in truth, she was excited about the Cooking Channel possibility. As she'd told Brady, for as long as she could remember, even before she'd met Jonathan, she'd dreamed of a cooking show on national TV. And now, he'd made it a possibility. She was grateful, so she chatted through lunch with him like nothing else was between them.

"I'm anxious to see *Wicked* tonight."

He smiled and this time it reached his eyes. "I am, too. It's hard to believe it's been out so long and we haven't seen it."

His intimate tone, his linking of their lives like this, made her uneasy again, so she was glad to see the food arrive.

Her grilled asparagus salad was wonderful and when she complimented it, Jonathan told the waiter who she was. The chef himself came out and said he was a fan of her cookbooks. It did her ego good, and she remembered how she'd savored her success, her fame, people recognizing her.

Maybe too much.

"I think we'll forgo dessert, if that's okay. I don't want to be late or spoil our dinner."

"Of course."

As they waited for the check, Jonathan asked, "Are you nervous?"

"No. But I remember how much I want this. I'm excited about it."

"Now that makes my day."

They took a cab through the city and when they reached the Madison Avenue offices of the Cooking Channel,

Jonathan helped her out of the car and, still holding her hand, whispered, "Ready to make all your dreams come true?"

She nodded, but her smile was forced. Because Jonathan didn't know that those dreams had been altered by her amnesia and what she'd learned about herself in the past six weeks. She still had some of them—like the one she was about to pursue—but basically, she was a different person.

BRADY STARED DOWN AT MILLIE and Raoul with a half smile. They were having a fight, and it didn't take Freud to figure out where this bend in the story had come from. Hell, was no aspect of his life safe from Clare?

He sketched Millie, the cuddly little mouse with soulful eyes, a scowl on her snout and her paws on her hips. "Don't badger me."

"I'm a rat, not a badger," Raoul responded sourly.

"Clacker is *my* friend, even if you don't like him."

"We don't need friends. We have each other."

Arrgh… Brady should just rip up this storyboard. It was going nowhere, and he'd let his personal life distract him from his work.

He was just about to tear the page out of his sketch pad when the doorbell rang. Hmm, who'd visit in the afternoon and not let himself in? Delia or Max would just come inside. Maybe Donny, Brady thought hopefully. He was always open to spending time with the kid, and sometimes Dee let him come up alone. They often talked about Millie and Raoul, so maybe Donny could help him think of another tack to take besides one that mirrored Brady's personal life.

He pulled open the door and was shocked to see Lucinda on the other side. Her pretty reddish-brown hair was a mass of waves down her back, and she was dressed in white pants and a black-and-white shirt that showed off her body. "Hi, handsome."

"Lucy, this is a surprise."

She arched an auburn brow. "Didn't you get my messages? I said I might stop by today."

Shifting from one foot to the other, he felt like a kid in front of the principal. "Um, yeah. Things have been hectic. Come on in."

She stepped into his condo. "I went with Sam last night to visit your mom. She's doing well."

"Well enough to kick me out."

Go home, honey. Work things out there.

I don't know if there's anything to work out there, Mom.

Well, you can't hide here forever.

Who says?

Your mother, who loves you.

"Brady?"

"Come into the living room."

Taking a seat on his couch, which faced the back of the apartment, Lucinda patted the cushion next to her. "I thought we might spend some time together. I have the afternoon off."

Lucinda ran a successful boutique in the city specializing in yoga wear. He'd met her there when he was buying a birthday present for his sister Juliana.

"What did you have in mind?" he asked after he joined her. He didn't feel like going out with her, but he was also bummed about Clare being in New York with Harris.

"Now, there's a question."

Uh-oh. He hadn't said that to be flirty. God, the last thing he felt like doing was…

"Don't look so grim. I'm not going to seduce you…yet."

"Lucy, things just aren't the same for me now."

"I know." Her expression was sympathetic. She was a nice woman. "You've been involved in helping Clare, which I think is admirable since she did such a number on you."

Thank you, Sam, for talking out of turn.

"And I know you're exhausted from helping your mom. I thought an afternoon at the Little Theater for a Fellini film, then dinner at Síbon, might be fun."

When he still hesitated, she gave him a sultry look. "All right, I'll be honest. I know you're backing away from this relationship. I can sense it. But I don't want that. So, for now, I'll settle for being together, no demands, no worries."

He was about to decline when he caught sight of a picture of him and Clare on the table. He didn't want to sit here, wondering about how the Cooking Channel interview was going, or whether she was seeing a Broadway show with Harris, or worse, where she was staying tonight. Even though she'd told him she wouldn't sleep with Jonathan, he was agonizing over the fact that she could change her mind.

"You know what? I think going to the movies is a great idea." He stood. "Give me time to change."

She indicated his jeans and casual shirt. "You look fine." She smiled. "I like you as you are."

Nice to hear. "I want to dress up a bit. Make yourself at home."

He left her alone in the living room and headed for the shower. He'd always liked Lucy's forthrightness and her sense of fun. But he'd forgotten that she made him feel good about who he was. Today, he needed that.

THEY SAT ON LEATHER COUCHES in the huge office of the CEO of the Cooking Channel, one befitting Abe Lewis's stature. Up twenty flights, the space overlooked Madison Avenue through a huge set of windows, was beautifully appointed with teak accents and, if Jonathan guessed correctly, featured a real Monet landscape on the wall.

Lewis was a tall, imposing man with a corporate smile. "It's good to finally have the chance to meet you, Ms. Boneli." There was an undercurrent in his tone and Clarissa seemed to catch it, as did Jonathan.

"You, too, Mr. Lewis. I'm sorry about having to cancel our previous meeting. I'm afraid it was a family emergency and I simply couldn't leave town."

Family, my ass, Jonathan thought, feeling the familiar anger rise in him. The Langstons were *not* her family and never would be, if he had his way. Brady Langston was *not* going to win her back. Jonathan had had a lot of time to think over the past week, and he realized Clarissa was trying to put distance between them. He'd resolved to do whatever he had to in order to keep her. Because of the accident, he had a second chance, and he intended to make the most of it. This appointment was a start.

"In any case," Lewis said flatly, "let's get right to the meat of the matter. I've viewed the tapes Jonathan sent me and can see, with a few changes, how your show might very well fit into our lineup."

Looking chic and sophisticated, Clarissa kept her cool but showed the right amount of enthusiasm. "I'm glad to hear that. You won't be surprised to know it's always been a dream of mine to be on the Cooking Channel."

Jonathan stared at the tasteful matted and framed posters

on the far wall: Ramona Rich, Claudia Dean. Soon, Clarissa Boneli would be among them.

"Then we're on the same page."

"I hope so."

He frowned. "Excuse me?"

"I'd like to know what changes you'd be making."

"Oh, well, of course." He shot a questioning look at Jonathan. Rarely would anybody pass up a chance to go national, no matter what changes Lewis suggested.

"Our Clarissa is a perfectionist," Jonathan said smoothly, trying to cover up for her, even though he was shocked himself that she hadn't immediately consented.

Lewis picked up a folder on his desk and opened it. "My team has some minor things. We'd probably change the name of the show. Something a bit more...Italian. Maybe the *Italian Princess*."

The line between Clarissa's brows told Jonathan she didn't like the title but she said, "I guess a name change wouldn't be so bad. What else?"

"Listed here is a new set, a bit fancier."

A genuine smile this time. "I don't care about the set. As long as it has a stove, a sink and a cooktop."

Lewis gave her a few other minor suggestions that, thankfully, didn't mean anything to her.

When the executive leaned back in his chair with a glint in his eye, Jonathan knew what was coming. "The last request is a bit more significant. We'd want some...partnership, I guess you'd say, in your cookbooks."

"In my cookbooks? Why? What do they have to do with the show?"

"When you syndicate, everything's about the show. This is the big leagues, Clarissa. We couldn't have you going off on your own with the cookbooks while we're promoting your name across the country—the world, actually. We'd be creating an image for every aspect of your professional life."

She crossed her legs and leaned back. "I don't know if I can agree to this."

"No offense, Clarissa...may I call you that?"

"Yes, Abe, you can."

"The books need updating." He pulled out pictures of the covers. "This format has served you well to get you established, but some changes would increase sales, I think."

She cocked her head. "I thought they were selling well."

"Our shows, and their ancillary products, are promoted aggressively. To fit into that market, these need to be...a bit more chic."

"I see. I'd be glad to talk about this further, when my illustrator can be present."

"I don't think that will be necessary, Clarissa."

"Why?"

"Because one of the things that would have to go are the illustrations."

"SHALL WE ORDER ANOTHER bottle?" Lucy asked from across the small table at Síbon, a dimly lit, crowded little restaurant on Park Avenue.

Brady knew he shouldn't have more wine, though they'd taken a cab to the movies and walked to the restaurant from there. But he wasn't much of a drinker, and they'd already killed a bottle.

"No thanks. I'm done."

She arched her brows. "Aren't you having fun?"

"I am. I'm glad you suggested this."

"I'm good for you, Brady."

He guessed that was true. He'd forgotten it, in light of what had happened with Clare. Now, though, she had part of her memory back, and maybe, in New York tonight, she would get the rest.

The thought of her sleeping with Jonathan—or worse, her having slept with him the night of the accident, after she'd been with Brady—made him ill. A sense of despair came out of nowhere. What if she did remember everything and wanted Jonathan again like the last time, and was upset with Brady for their lovemaking? He had to swallow back the painful emotion in his gut.

So he said, "You know what? I changed my mind. We'll have more wine." He raised his hand to call the waiter. "Bring another bottle." If Clare being away with another man wasn't enough to drive him to drink, nothing was.

"That's the Brady I know and love."

Reaching across the table, he took Lucinda's hand. "Thanks for asking me to come out, Lucy. I needed this."

"I'm not giving up on you, Brady."

Oh-oh. Geez, he wished he didn't have to be fair. But it was part of his makeup. "Luce, I don't want to lead you on. Things have changed for me."

"Yes, I know. But they can change back, given the right circumstances. For us." She arched a brow. "And for Clare."

Could Clare be changing back this very moment into the Clarissa who'd dumped him?

When more wine was poured, he lifted his glass and took a swig. Then another. And another. Soon it dulled his despair, which was all he wanted tonight.

SHE WAITED UNTIL THEIR early dinner at the revolving restaurant in the Marriott was over, and before they went to the theater, to say to Jonathan, "We need to talk."

Casually, he leaned back in his chair and looked out the floor-to-ceiling windows. The restaurant had already revolved once, giving them a spectacular view of the city.

"I know what you're going to ask. No, I didn't know about the changes Lewis suggested. No, I didn't know he thought your image could be more chic. And, no, I didn't arrange to have him cut Langston out of the cookbooks."

"Did you know that he wanted a hand in the cookbooks?"

Jonathan flushed and averted his gaze, a neon sign that answered her question. "Yes." Picking up his wineglass, he sipped his merlot.

"Why didn't you tell me before I went to the meeting? Prepare me? I was totally ambushed in there."

"Because," he said in a harsh whisper, anger alight in his eyes, "I didn't think you'd come to New York to see him if you knew how much control he wanted. The old Clarissa would have, but since you lost your memory, I can't depend on what you're going to do."

"Well, you would have been right. I wouldn't have come to New York if it meant cutting Brady out of the books. And I resent the fact that you tricked me."

Frowning, he looked around. "Keep your voice down."

"I'll do more than that." Angry, she threw her napkin on the table, stood and walked away without another word.

She reached the elevator while Jonathan was presumably paying the bill, rode it to the sixteenth floor and found her way to her room. Purposely she opened the connecting door from her side and found his already ajar. She paced until she heard him come into the room and appear in the doorway.

"What the hell were you doing, leaving like that?"

She rounded on him. His face was flushed. Jonathan didn't get angry very often, but as she'd known before, and witnessed since the accident, anything to do with Brady set him off. "I'm furious with you," she said.

"I can tell."

"You had no right to lie to me."

"No right? You wouldn't even be considered for the Cooking Channel if it wasn't for me."

"Oh, and here I thought it was my talent that got me this far."

He stood ramrod straight, his expression tight. "And my connections."

"You were very wrong to do this, Jonathan."

"Damn it." His voice rose considerably. "Do you have any idea what kind of opportunity this is? How rare an offer you've gotten? The old Clarissa would have jumped at the chance no matter what was asked of her."

Squaring her shoulders, Clare crossed the rug and stood in front of him. "I know she would have."

"You…" The expression on his face went from anger, to surprise, to something else she couldn't decipher. This close, she could see him redden again. "Does that mean what I think it means?"

"I have my memory back."

His complexion drained of color. Why? "All of it?"

Her shoulders sagged. "No, not all. I still can't remember the two hours before the accident. But pretty much everything else."

He swallowed hard. "What *do* you remember about that night?"

Facing him like this was…familiar. Frightening. Suddenly she started to tremble and her head began to hurt. He reached for her but she stepped back. "Don't. We're going to have this out now, no matter how it makes me feel. And I want the truth. If you lie to me, I'll never forgive you."

"I won't lie."

"Did I come to your house the night of the accident? Around twelve?"

"Yes."

Clare deflated. "And all these weeks, you didn't tell me? Why?"

"Because I thought we weren't supposed to tell you everything outright. That if you were blocking experiences for psychological reasons, then it wasn't a good idea to reveal what I knew, but that I should let it come to the surface when you were ready." He scowled. "Hell, Clarissa, why do I have to defend myself here?"

She ignored the question. "What happened that night that I might block, Jonathan?"

He angled his chin. "Tell me what you remember, first."

Because she felt weak, she moved to sit on the bed. But damn it, she would see this through. "I came to you to tell you what I'd done."

"You mean that you slept with Langston."

So he did know. In some ways that was a huge relief. On the heels of that, anger surfaced. All these weeks, he'd known something this important and hadn't told her.

Then again, so had Brady. The thought diffused some of her resentment.

"That's all I remember."

"I...see."

She couldn't read his expression.

"What did you say when I told you?"

"More to the point is what else you said."

"Really?"

Covering the distance between them, he sat down next to her and took her hand. She hated his touching her, but she was feeling really sick, so she allowed it. "You said you felt guilty for betraying me. You said there was no making this up to me."

"I can believe all that. Did you kick me out? Did I leave upset and get in the accident?"

He hesitated. "I told you I forgave you. I told you I wanted to marry you."

Clare began to tremble again. Violently. "What? Then why did I leave?"

"I think it was the guilt. You felt so bad. I went to get you something to drink, and when I returned, you were gone. My car was in the shop, so I couldn't follow you."

Suddenly, Clare saw him there in his house, the one in the photo album and this time she remembered it...

"I LOVE YOU. I've always loved you. This doesn't change anything."

"No, no, you don't understand what's happened."

"We can work through this, love. We can work through anything."

"Jonathan..."

BEFORE SHE COULD remember more, her mind exploded with a blinding headache. Her hands went to her temples. "Oh!"

"Clarissa, honey, another headache? It must be because you remember the worst of it."

"I'm going to be sick." She rushed to the bathroom, dropped to her knees and vomited violently.

Eventually, she became conscious of Jonathan holding back her hair. Saying soothing words, telling her everything was going to be all right. Then, he drew her up, wiped her face and gave her a toothbrush. "There, there, Clarissa, it's over, it's all over…"

Clare awoke with a start. What? Where was she? It was pitch-black and she became aware of an eerie quiet in the room. *Stay calm. Breathe.* Those were Brady's words at the hospital, she remembered now.

Rolling over she looked at the lighted red numbers on the clock. 1:00 a.m. They'd missed *Wicked.* Because she'd remembered everything. She sighed, disturbed by what had been revealed tonight.

She'd gone over to Jonathan's, confessed to sleeping with another man and he'd forgiven her. Something didn't ring true, though. Why had his understanding been traumatic enough to blank out her memory? There was no reason to hide forgiveness.

Finally, she got up and made her way to the bathroom. The adjoining doors were still ajar and that little intimacy made her uncomfortable. Quickly, she closed her side, went into the bath and took a shower.

Once she was in pajamas with a towel wrapped around her head, she padded back to the bed. Feeling incredibly sad, she sat on the side, bare feet dangling to the floor, unable to figure out where the hopeless, lonely feeling was coming from.

She picked up the phone on the nightstand.

She needed to talk to Brady.

The operator connected her to his home phone, the one by the bed, in case he was asleep or his cell wasn't nearby. She was nervous but needed to hear his voice.

Four rings. She was about to give up when she heard a click, then, "Hello."

It wasn't Brady's voice. It was a feminine voice. A sleep-slurred feminine voice. And if Clare wasn't mistaken, it belonged to Lucinda Gray.

She slammed the phone down. Already furious with one man, she let the same feeling come about another. Goddamn it, had Brady slept with his girlfriend?

AN ALLIGATOR WAS BANGING at the closed door between her room and Jonathan's. It was so loud, so menacing, it scared Clare to death. She could hear it growl, picture its ugly teeth, its red eyes.

Lying on the bed, she burrowed deeper into the covers, unable to stop the battering, more frightened than she'd ever been in her life. The monster was going to get through.

Suddenly, she was bathed in green light. The whole room was. It created a bubble around her. In its warm glow, a calm feeling washed over her. She wanted to become part of the light, part of what was on this side of the door. Her heart ached with the need.

Bang, bang!

The door splintered.

More thrashing, then clawing, scratching. And growls so loud they hurt her ears.

She tried to hide her face, but the covers were whipped off her, and the green light, the secure green glow, evaporated.

Clare watched in horror as the snout of the huge animal

broke through the wood. His head inside, he looked around with his beady red eyes, his scaly skin glistening in the overhead lights. Then his jaws opened, baring sharp teeth. Then those jaws clacked shut, the sound reverberating in the still hotel room.

In that moment, Clare knew the thing was going to devour her.

CHAPTER FOURTEEN

AT FOUR THE NEXT afternoon, Clare took the elevator up to the second floor of the house and approached her doorway with a heavy heart and a still-queasy stomach. Getting sick last night had drained most of her energy, and what was left of it had been sucked out of her by the horrific dream. She'd awakened at dawn with a start and couldn't go back to sleep.

The dream had scared her, though she understood why she'd had it: she'd closed the doors between her room and Jonathan's, and they'd missed *Wicked,* hence the green. The alligator… Who the hell knew? She was getting tired of amateur psychology and wanted some peace.

When she reached her condo, she found a note tucked under the number. It read:

> I went to the zoo with Donny and Delia. I'll bring supper back. Can't wait to hear about New York. Cath.

Well, that was okay. Clare could use some time to digest everything. Her anger at Jonathan had been diluted this morning when he'd been kind and sensitive to her, giving her space, talking only when she wanted to. He'd apologized profusely for not having told her what he knew about the night of her accident, and Clare *did* understand his reasoning…

"PLEASE FORGIVE ME, Clare. I thought I was doing the right thing."

"I guess I know that."

Brady had kept it from her, too, and she could understand both men's reasoning, though she didn't like either.

"I need something from you, Clarissa."

"What?"

"Promise me you won't decide anything until this all sinks in, until you have time to internalize what you've found out."

She thought of Jonathan holding her head while she was sick last night, of the tender way he cradled her hand in his when she was scared. And how he'd forgiven her for sleeping with another man. She could give him a little more time, she guessed.

"All right. I won't make any decisions right now. I want to talk to Anna Summers about everything, anyway."

HE'D EVEN LEFT her off at home without asking to come up, without forcing any affection on her, thank God.

As she slid her key into the lock, she glanced next door. The birds made her smile, and she wanted to see Brady, badly, but she wouldn't go over there. First off, he could still be in bed with Lucinda, which just about leveled Clare. She knew from experience he was a lusty lover, and she bet he could spend all day in bed. The thought worsened the nauseous feeling in her stomach and made her eyes cloud.

She also had to find a way to tell him about the Cooking Channel. Not that she intended to leave him out of their books. The old Clare would have, but not her.

Inside, she headed straight for the bedroom. She dropped her bags on the floor when she saw Brady, stretched out on her bed facedown, sound asleep. Even in profile, he looked terrible—his jaw unshaven, and his color bad. He must have had a long night.

The thought made her sicker. Her sense of loss, of messing things up, of maybe losing him, had her crossing the room. She sat on the mattress and touched his back, smoothed her hand over it, enjoying the feel of his muscles, the contours of his body. His skin was tanned, as he liked to work outside without a shirt. His waist was narrow. His hair was mussed. Swallowing back regret, guilt and just plain frustration, she gently shook his shoulder. "Brade, wake up."

A blue eye opened. The first thing she noticed was it was bloodshot. He groaned, buried his face back in the pillow.

"Brady?" she said gently.

Finally, he rolled over and opened both eyes. Focused. "Clare, what?"

"You're in my bedroom."

He arched his back as if it was sore. "What time is it?"

"Four."

"In the afternoon?"

"Uh-huh. I'm back from New York."

"Wow." He ran a hand through his hair, making it stick up. "I came here about noon to wait for you. Sorry, I fell asleep."

Which gave her an indication of how tired he must have been. She watched him. "Rough night?"

"Yeah. Really rough."

"And wild?" She couldn't keep the sadness out of her voice. She tried, but thinking of him with Lucinda made her desperate. And then a thought struck her: Oh dear Lord, was this how it had been for Brady all the months she'd been with Jonathan? No wonder he'd been angry and hurt.

"Excuse me?"

What the hell? She was going to tell him everything anyway. "I called you at 2:00 a.m. Lucinda answered the phone."

"Why didn't she wake me?"

"I hung up."

"Why did you call?"

She waited. "I was alone and scared. I remembered pretty much everything last night. Jonathan and I had a terrible fight, and I got violently ill."

"Oh, sweetheart, I'm sorry. You do look pale." He touched her arm. "What did you fight about?"

"I'll tell you in a minute. First I need to know something. Did you sleep with Lucinda?"

"*What?*"

"Are you seeing her again? Sleeping with her?"

He sat up and stuffed pillows behind his head. "Did you stay with Harris in New York?"

"I said I was alone when I called."

He arched a brow. "That's not an answer."

"No, I didn't sleep with him. I told you I wouldn't. Why won't anybody *listen* to me?"

"Is that what you fought about?"

"Partly. What about Lucinda?"

"She came over without me inviting her. I was bummed about your going to New York with Harris. We went out, and I had more than three glasses of wine."

A small smile graced her lips. "Uh-oh."

"You remember what happens when I do that?"

"I've put you to bed more than once because you had more than three glasses of anything."

"I didn't sleep with her. She stayed, but nothing happened."

"I see."

"Your turn. Tell me about Harris."

She picked at her coverlet, trying to let the warm breeze coming in through the window calm her. "I told Jonathan I remembered going to his house. I asked him what happened when I was there."

"That's a new piece—remembering you went to his house."

"Yes, after a nudge, some of it came back to me. He told me a little bit, then the whole thing was just there for me. At least I think it was the whole thing. In some ways it still doesn't make a lot of sense."

Brady was fully awake and staring at her intently. "What doesn't make sense?"

"I know I went to his house, really upset. I remember telling him that I slept with you."

"Holy hell. Did he flip out?"

"I guess not. He said he took the news calmly. I don't remember that part, just me telling him about us. He said he told me he forgave me and asked me to marry him."

"*What?*" When she didn't say more, he asked, "Damn it, Clare, did you…did you say yes?"

"No. He said I didn't give him an answer, then I left when he went to get me something to drink."

"Why did you leave if he was so understanding?" There was suspicion in his tone and on his face. Rightfully so.

"He said I felt so guilty for sleeping with you that I couldn't accept his forgiveness."

"How convenient for him."

"Why the sarcasm?"

"If he was so forgiving, why didn't he go look for you?"

"His car was in the shop."

"He could have called somebody." Brady's face tightened. "I can't believe he just let you go off like that by yourself. What kind of a jerk is he?"

"Brady, he was upset because I slept with you."

"He should have put your welfare first."

Which was what Brady would have done, had always done.

"And why the hell didn't he tell you all this before, if what happened was so innocuous?"

"Like you, he said he thought it was better to let me remember on my own."

Brady looked chagrined. "I guess the pot can't call the kettle black." Reaching over, he squeezed her hand. "It's still hard for me to believe his benign acceptance of what you told him would make you run out of there. Make you forget everything."

"We were never sure the amnesia was psychological. Maybe it's simply a long-term reaction to the head injury."

"Again, that seems coincidental." He sighed and scrutinized her face. "How are you feeling now?"

She shook her head. "It's so odd, Brady, now that my memory's returned. I remember the old Clare from before with you, and the new Clare, too. Right now, I don't know which one I am."

He slid off the bed and stood. "You don't have to know yet. When's your next appointment with Anna?"

"Early Monday."

"You can get at some of this stuff then." He tried to pull her up. "Come on, let's go get me a Coke for this hangover, and you can tell me about the Cooking Channel."

Her eyes filled with tears.

Squatting in front of her, his grip tightened. "What happened, sweetheart—didn't you get the offer?"

"No, I got it."

"Why are you crying?"

"The executives want to make changes in everything."

"The show can withstand that," he said neutrally.

"Not just in the show." She stared at his wonderful face, knowing her next words were going to hurt him, badly. "They want rights over the cookbooks."

"Why the hell would they care about our books?"

Our books. "That's just it, Brade. They don't want you to illustrate them anymore."

"They want me out?"

Her throat filled with emotion, she could only nod.

He let loose a crude expletive. "Did Harris engineer this?"

"No, but he knew about it."

"I'll just bet he did." His face blanked. "Did you?"

"Of course not!" She blew out a heavy breath. "It's a moot point, anyway. I'm not going to meet their demands."

He waited a long time, searching her face, before he said, "You have to. In order to realize your dream, you have to leave me out of it, Clare."

WITH A COKE IN HAND, sitting on Clare's bar stool, Brady reiterated his earlier statement. "You're going to accept the network's offer." It wasn't a question. She needed to do this, with or without him. The ramifications were untenable, but she had to do what was best for her. He loved her enough to face the issue.

"Brady, I'm not going to stop working with you on our books." She shook her head hard. "I don't want to."

"I won't stand in your way. You've always dreamed about being on national TV, even when you were the old Clare. You talked about it all the time."

"I told you, in some ways I am the old Clare, and I won't do this to you. To us."

"It's not your choice."

"Of course it is. And I've made it."

He ignored her comment. "We'll finish this last cookbook, then you can go on to bigger and better things."

"Brady—"

"My agent will be overjoyed. I can accept the offer from Random House for a new series. Remember I told you about it? It's for mega bucks."

"Please, don't make plans like this. At least not now. Besides, you don't care about the money."

"No, I care about you. This is settled." When she just stared at him, he asked the question that had been on his mind since she'd told him what she'd remembered. "Now, I need to know something else. What are you going to do about Harris?"

She actually looked torn, and it kicked him in the gut. Dear God, was she going to reject him again?

"Like you said, I need to talk to Anna, give myself time to figure out how things are. Some pieces that night still don't make sense. I can't make any big decisions about anything yet, Brady."

"This is his doing, isn't it?"

She shrugged a shoulder, like she did when she didn't want to admit something.

"Clare?"

"All right, he asked me to promise him one thing—not to make any decisions right away. To let it all sink in, internalize everything that's happened to me."

"And you said yes?"

"Of course I did. I owe him that much."

"You owe him nothing."

"Brady, I told you before that I can't continue living my life by alienating people I care about. I don't want to be that person again."

It was déjà vu. He remembered vividly how the course of events had played out last time. "This is so familiar, Clare. It's what he did initially. Asked for little things, a bit more of your time. To skip movie night. To push deadlines on the books so you could do the show. And the same thing will happen. He'll lure you in with Lewis's offer, get you back in his clutches, like he did the last time with the local show. Then he'll talk you into moving in with him."

"No, no, he won't."

"It's already happening. You're letting him start down the same road a second time."

"No, I'm not. I just said I'd give myself some time. Which I need, Brady. For myself, too." When he didn't respond, she added, "You said this morning I should talk to Anna before I made any decisions."

"This is different."

"Brady, please."

He ignored her statement again. "I've been here before, Clare." He shook his head forcefully. "I can't watch this happen all over again. It almost killed me the first time."

Her face revealed utter panic. "No, I can't lose you, either. I know that."

"Sweetheart, it was always going to come to this. Him or me. And you said you couldn't choose."

"But Brady..."

He stood because he had to get out of her kitchen. He felt his resolve slipping, felt as if he might let her sacrifice the show for him and stay in her life, no matter whom she chose. And he loved her too much to do that.

He also couldn't do it to himself a second time. If she wasn't going to choose to be with him, any kind of relationship with Clare was impossible.

"I'm leaving. Call Harris and tell him you're going to do what Lewis asked. He'll be happy." Brady leaned over and kissed her cheek. "Goodbye, Clare. I'll send over the drawings when they're done for the rest of the book. You have enough to finish it on your own."

"I can't believe this. It sounds so final."

"Because it is."

Quietly, Brady let himself out of the condo. Once in the hall, he leaned against the door and closed his eyes. Somewhere in his heart, he'd been hoping she'd make a different decision. When he'd told her their professional and personal lives would be over, he'd been praying she'd choose him, right now, on the spot. But she hadn't. Her wavering was the same thing she'd done before. And he meant what he said—he was pretty sure things would go down the way they had then, too.

This time, he wouldn't stick around for it. Watch it happen, as he'd told her. He'd done what was best for Clare—and for himself, given the circumstances—and it was time to get on with his life without Clarissa Boneli in it.

On Monday morning, before her appointment with Anna, Clare pulled up to the curb at the Rockford Airport and looked over at Cathy. "You sure you don't want me to come in?"

"Of course not. You can't go through security and wait with me, so it's stupid to park the car." She reached over to grab Clare's hand. "You look so sad. I hate to leave. But I've got commitments."

"I know. It's okay. I have to stand on my own sometime." Without Cathy, without Brady. Now that Clare had her memory back, she knew how much she'd depended on him in the past.

"Listen, Cath, I want to say one thing, before you go. I'm sorry for drifting away from you. I'm never, *ever* going to do that again, no matter what happens. I promise."

Cathy smiled. "It's in the past. We're making a new start."

"I know. I love you."

Cathy kissed her cheek. "I love you, too."

Again, with a heavy heart, Clare watched her sister go into the airport terminal. She sat there, staring after Cathy until a horn beeped behind the car. She pulled out of the space and drove downtown to Anna's office. In some ways she was looking forward to the session, hoping for more clarity, and in some ways she was dreading it.

After Clare recounted the return of her memory and what she'd learned about that horrid night, Anna was matter-of-fact. "Let's take this one step at a time. First, I'm glad you got most of your memory back. But you really don't remember everything about that night. You said so yourself that not all the pieces fit together. After you told Jonathan what happened with Brady, there are still some blanks. You don't remember leaving his house or the accident?"

"That's right. But he told me what happened."

"Which you should recall, and you don't. Second, I'm not clear on what actually sent you running out into the night."

"Jonathan says it was my guilt. For betraying him."

"But we don't know that for sure and won't until all of it comes back to you."

"So you think there's more?"

"My gut tells me there might be. I haven't wanted to

push you too hard, so I haven't brought this up before, but there's another possibility and I think we should get it out in the open. Could it be that, after you told Jonathan what happened with Brady, he forced some intimacy on you?"

"I don't know what you mean. He held me, I remember crying in his arms but... Oh, God, do you mean did we... No, oh, Lord, I can't believe I'd do that." She felt the worst bout of panic she'd had yet well up inside her and push against her chest. "I couldn't have been with another man that same night. I wouldn't do that, Anna. Not even as the Clare I became."

"Calm down. I don't mean that I think you did. It's just that I've considered this as a possible reason that your memory is blocked. Also, Cathy called me before she left. She said she and Brady discussed the same thing but were afraid to bring it up."

"She and Brady discussed *this?*" Her heart pounded. Her hands felt clammy. "Brady thinks I did this? No wonder he was so upset."

"He thinks it's a possibility. Everybody's just worried that this could be the traumatic event that caused your amnesia."

Taking deep breaths, Clare forced herself to calm down and began to think more clearly. "It's not a possibility. I wouldn't have done that."

"Even if he coerced you."

"*He* wouldn't have done that. Jonathan loves me, Anna. He wouldn't do something so terrible to me."

"A man faced with losing the woman he loves often acts out of character."

"No, I don't believe it."

"Then we're still in the dark about the rest."

"If there is more." Clare was thoughtful. "You said

sometimes people don't get all their memories back. Maybe I'll never know if there was more."

"Or maybe you'll make life-altering decisions without knowing what really happened, and then the past will come back to bite you in the butt when you least expect it."

"Anna, *I'm* not making these decisions. Brady is. He left the last of the drawings at my door yesterday. I'll be finishing the book myself."

"Did you try to talk to him again?"

"Of course. I went right over to his place. He answered the door, but wouldn't let me in." She told the counselor what had happened.

"YOU GOT THE DRAWINGS?"

"Yes. I found them just now."

"Good. What do you want?"

"I can't let things end like this. I won't."

He drew in a deep breath. "Clare, baby, if you care anything at all about me, then you'll accept my decision. It's the decent thing to do. I can't prevent you from having what you've dreamed of all your life. And maybe you and Harris belong together. You care about him."

She wanted to lie. But she couldn't. "I remember caring about Jonathan. But I love you, Brady."

"Not enough to choose me. Right now. Please, Clare, go. Please…"

WHEN SHE FINISHED THE STORY, Anna said simply, "That makes *me* sad. What are you going to do?"

"Nothing, I guess. I do care enough about him to let him go."

"And he cares enough about you to let you go. What's wrong with this picture, Clare?"

She shook her head.

"All right, time's almost up. I want to say two more things. I suggest you don't do anything about the TV show until I see you again." She checked her calendar. "How about on Wednesday?"

They set a time.

"What else?" Clare asked.

"As I said before, I'm not really into dream symbolism as a method of treating patients, but your New York dream, it's fraught with metaphor."

"I thought it was a mixture of reality and fantasy." She told Anna about the adjoining doors and the green theme in *Wicked*.

"It is reality and fantasy—maybe fear, too—colliding. In classic dream interpretation, the alligator is a sign of an aggressor, the locked door indicative of something you don't want to remember, and the green—that you were bathed in—a need for harmony."

"You're not telling me Jonathan was the alligator."

"No, Clare, I believe *you* just told *me* that."

AT NOON ON MONDAY, MAX and Delia came barging through Brady's door like a posse looking for its prey. Max's face was tight with anger, and Delia looked as if she'd been crying.

"What the hell is this?" Max asked, holding up the wooden sign.

Brady sighed. Where was he going to get the energy to deal with them? "Exactly what it looks like. I was planning to tell you as soon as you got back. I didn't know the real estate agent had put that up already."

Grasping his arm, Delia held on tight. "Brady, please, you can't sell your condo."

"I have to."

Max threw the sign down on the floor. "It's because of Clare, isn't it?"

He knew it would cause World War Three, but Brady was done lying, covering up, fooling them as well as himself. "Yes."

Delia turned to Max. "Clare has her memory back."

Max had just returned from his trip the night before. "Then all this makes sense." He began to pace. "Obviously, she's turned into the selfish bitch she was before she got amnesia. I knew she would."

"That's not true. She seems to be a little of both the old and new Clare." Delia pointed to the sign on the floor. "Brady, what happened to precipitate this? The day before she went to New York, the day Donny came home, you two were closer than I'd seen you in a long time."

He blew out a heavy breath. "Sit down, there are some things I've been keeping from you."

They sat as they had a thousand times on his stuffed couches, and he related the whole sordid story, only leaving out intimate details. The events infuriated Max further, and Delia started to cry again.

"He's won," Brady said. "He's got her back."

"And she just took the damn deal in New York? Leaving you behind?" Max shook his head. "I was right all along, she doesn't deserve you."

"No, she hasn't taken it. She says she won't, because of me."

Delia nodded knowingly. "And you can't live with that?"

"No, I can't deprive her of her lifelong dream. Nor can

I live here and watch her and Jonathan get together like they did the last time. It's why I'm selling this place. I'm going to New York to live for a while. My agent's thrilled."

Max's black eyes flamed. "What about us?"

"I'm sorry, Max. I just don't know how else to get through this."

"All I can say is she better move out, too. I won't stay if she does."

"She will. Harris had a house picked out for them before the accident."

Delia hugged Brady. "It seems so unfair. Like a tease. We had a chance to get her back, and now it's gone. I know it's worse for you."

"I'll live. And, Dee, I'll talk to Donny when he gets back from his friend's house today. I'll see him at least once a month. I'd stay for him if I could, but I just can't."

"Are you going to wait until this place sells?" Max asked.

"No, I've got a flight out tonight to New York. I'll be at Charlie's place." Where the four of them had always stayed in the past, where they had a history. "But I want my whereabouts kept from Clare."

"I can't believe this, bro."

Brady shrugged. "Me, either."

CLARE WALKED AROUND DOWNTOWN for an hour after her appointment with Anna. She had so much to think about, primarily the fact that she might not be remembering everything. But nothing came to her; there was absolutely no recollection of anything else that might have happened that night.

She remained resolute, though, that Anna—and Cathy and Brady, for God's sake—were wrong. Jonathan wouldn't have forced her or shamed her into any kind of intimacy. In her heart, she knew that. But as she walked and window-shopped, ate lunch and sat in the park, she kept thinking about Anna's assertion that something was missing.

As Clare herself had suggested, though, maybe she would never remember.

By the end of the afternoon, she'd come to a few conclusions.

Despite Brady's protest, she wasn't going to take the Cooking Channel deal. She wouldn't sell her proverbial soul to the proverbial devil for success. She knew she could never do that to Brady.

She loved him. Really, truly loved him.

Yet, she cared about Jonathan, too, though not in the same way. And until she figured out what was what, and maybe remembered the rest of that night, she'd take her time and let Anna help her. As the counselor had suggested, she was sticking to her guns and not making any commitment or changes in her life.

At about five, she felt good enough to go back home. She'd be honest—she'd tell Brady and Jonathan the conclusions she'd come to. She'd convince them both to give her time. If they really loved her, they'd do what she asked.

"WHAT CAN I DO FOR YOU, Langston?" Harris had been shocked when Brady had called and asked to see him. Brady could hear it in his voice. He'd tried to put Brady off, but when he'd told Harris he was leaving town tonight, the guy had acquiesced. Which had brought him to Harris's office to do one last thing.

"I need to say a few things," Brady told him, sticking his hands into his jeans because he was nervous. "And I have a question."

Dressed in a great-looking suit, Harris sat down in a chair and indicated Brady should take the couch. "Shoot."

Brady sat. "The question first." Man, this was hard. But he had to know some things before he left. "Clare remembers coming to your house that night."

"And which night would that be? The night you seduced her?"

"I...I'm sorry we did that to you." He was, really. "It was wrong."

"You're damn right it was wrong."

"I want to know what happened after she told you about us."

"Why would I tell you this, if Clare didn't?"

"She did tell me. What she remembers of it. But I need to know before I leave town if you did something that might make her lose her memory."

The guy looked guilty. Damn, was it true, then?

But Harris said only, "What are you getting at?"

"Did you insist she sleep with you? To prove she was sorry for being with me, like she said she was?"

Leaping out of the chair, Harris lunged at Brady. He grabbed him by the collar, dragged him up and got in his face. "You son of a bitch. I love her. I'd never do something like that to her."

Brady let out a heavy breath. There was no way Harris's reaction was faked. It eased the fist around his heart. "That," he said, shrugging off the guy's hold, "makes what I'm doing a lot easier."

Harris backed up a step and straightened his suit, obviously trying to calm himself. "What are you doing?"

"I'm leaving town."

"So you said."

"For good. Clare's still confused, but I don't think she'll take the Cooking Channel deal if I'm in the picture."

"That would be my guess. So you're bowing out?"

Brady nodded.

"Why?"

"Because I love her as much as you do." Brady swallowed hard, his throat convulsing. He loved her more, he was sure, but he didn't need another ruckus.

It took a minute to gather himself, then Brady crossed to the door. Just before he walked out, he turned around. "Take care of her, Jonathan."

EMOTIONALLY EXHAUSTED FROM what had been revealed over the past few days, from her therapy session and from the weight of the decisions she'd made today, Clare pulled into her driveway and got out of the car. As she headed up to the porch, she stopped short on the sidewalk. There was a For Sale sign in front of the house. She wondered if Max was moving out.

Or...no, no! She raced up the steps, let herself in and banged on Delia's door. No answer.

Then she went to Max's. No answer there, either.

Hurrying upstairs, she opened Brady's condo with her key to find no one there. She knew the place was empty, could feel the lack of his presence. A very bad feeling assaulted her. She checked his bathroom and saw toiletries were missing; she walked around, her anxiety escalating. Brady was gone. On a pass by the window, she caught sight of Max and Delia outside.

She hurried downstairs and out to the yard.

They were perched on top of the picnic table, feet on

the bench, each holding a beer. Each looking forlorn. And when they saw her, both their expressions turned hard.

"What's going on?" she asked, though by God she knew.

Dee spoke. "Brady's gone."

"Where is he?"

"He asked us not to tell you."

"Are you kidding? I need to stop him from leaving."

Max stood and straightened to his six-foot-plus height. "I've never felt less like kidding in my life. And why are you surprised? You drove him away. Again. But this time, he left us, too. We were fools to believe you'd changed, Clare, or would change. Brady's wised up, and so have we. We're done with you. Leave us all alone. It's the only decent thing to do."

She shot a panicky glance to Delia. "You, too, Dee?"

Delia's eyes were dry, but Clare could tell she'd been crying. "Yes, Clarissa, me, too."

CHAPTER FIFTEEN

THE WEEK AFTER BRADY LEFT was a nightmare. Clare had been unable to sleep Monday and Tuesday nights, wondering where Brady was, worrying about him, and feeling devastated by Max's and Delia's rejection. Every time she saw the For Sale sign on the lawn, she was heartbroken all over again. But when prospective buyers came to look at the apartment, reality sank in. Brady was gone.

Anna had a lot to say about that when Clare saw her on Wednesday. "Clare, let's suppose you don't ever discover all that happened that night, if indeed there is more. What do you—the woman you are right now, with the memories you have—want to happen?"

She told Anna what she'd decided on her afternoon alone after the last session. That she cared about both Brady and Jonathan, and that she needed time to make a decision. But even that was changing in the wake of Brady leaving. She knew deep down that she couldn't live her life without him. She simply couldn't.

"Hmm. I believe it's possible to love two men at once. But you obviously can't have them both. If you had to pick right now, today, who would you want to be with?"

"It doesn't matter. Brady's gone."

"You could get him to come back."

"Max and Delia, and Brady himself, said the only decent thing to do was leave him alone."

"What does Clare think?"

"Clare's a wreck and doesn't know what to do."

Anna chuckled at their lapse into third person, though at times over the past few months, she had felt as if she was talking about someone else. "Then I'll reiterate what I said last time. Clare should just lie low for a while."

Still, when Clare left the office, she was bereft.

Unexpected solace came on Thursday, when Lillian Langston called and asked her to come over to visit. Clare was so glad to see Brady's mother that she burst into tears when they met on her porch.

Generous like her son, Lillian hugged her. "Oh, honey, don't cry."

Clare drew back and swiped at her face. "Has he called? Do you know where he is?"

"He's called, but he doesn't want me to tell anyone where he is."

Biting her lip, Clare was ashamed to face Brady's mother. "Not anyone. Just me. He doesn't want to see me."

"That would be my guess."

Lillian linked their arms and they went around back and sat at an umbrella table Brady had bought for his mother. July had turned hot, especially in the afternoons. Clare tried to take pleasure in the profusion of colorful flowers surrounding the cement patio, but she couldn't. The sight of the hammock, of the yard, reminded her of good times she'd spent here with Brady. "Are you angry at me, Lillian?"

"No, not now. But I was when you got involved with Jonathan Harris."

"Join the club."

"*That* Clare hurt a lot of people."

"I hate that Clare."

"You do?"

"Yes, I'm not her anymore. I have some of her good traits, but I'm more like who I was before I got so...famous."

"She was the woman Brady loved."

Hearing that hurt. "What I've done is irreparable." Then she colored. His mother didn't know what had transpired between her and Brady.

"I know the gist of what happened, dear. Brady came here when he couldn't handle the events alone. But I'm not sure what you've done is beyond repair."

"What do you mean?"

"I've always thought that very little between men and women is irreparable. Brady's father and I went through some things the kids don't know about. And we survived. I think your problem is you haven't really made a choice."

"Why did you ask me here, Lillian?"

"Brady called and wanted me to check on you."

Clare buried her face in her hands. "Oh, God."

"And I'm alone tonight, Clare."

For Lillian's sake, she pulled herself together. "Really? Have you stayed alone yet, since you got home?"

"Yes, I have. But I'd like you to stay with me tonight."

"Why?"

"For company. And so I can keep an eye on you. I think it would be good for us both."

"All right. I'll run home and get a few things."

"No need. There's stuff here."

After a nice dinner that Clare prepared, and some idle

chitchat, Lillian showed her into Brady's room. That *stuff* she'd alluded to earlier turned out to be one of Brady's T-shirts, a toothbrush and toiletries in his bathroom upstairs, and his bed for the night.

When she saw all his things, she whispered, "Lillian, I'm not sure this is a good idea."

"You need to rest, dear. You'll sleep better in here."

"I—"

"Shh. Just go to sleep now."

"All right."

But it wasn't all right as she put on Brady's T-shirt, crawled into Brady's old bed, pulled up his quilt and buried her face in his pillow. Quite simply, Clare was miserable.

BRADY TOOK THE STAIRS DOWN to the pub he was temporarily living above in the Village. He was meeting his agent; they were celebrating tonight. Charlie was behind the long mahogany bar, washing glasses. Though his sons ran the place now, the old man still helped out.

"Hey there, Brady." Charlie angled his chin. "Leo is over by the window."

"You doing okay?"

"Getting by. Thanks to you."

Brady found his way to Leo, who hadn't lost the glow from their meeting with Random House this afternoon.

"Hey, Leo."

When Brady sat, Leo nodded to Charlie. "The old man looks good."

"Yeah."

"He thanked me for the clients I sent his way."

Years ago, when Charlie had been struggling to keep the pub afloat, he'd had the idea to make the upstairs into two suites to rent out. Brady, Max and Dee had stayed here whenever they could, and Leo had recommended the place to people he knew. Luckily for Brady, one of the spots had been empty this month.

Leo's shrewd gaze rested on Brady. "Though I'm not sure you should be staying here now."

"I know." There were a lot of memories in the place.

"You hear from her?"

"Nope. It's over. *Finis.* She's probably celebrating the Cooking Channel deal with Harris."

"Forget about it. We've got our own deal to celebrate."

Brady's grin was genuine. "I know. I can't believe they offered me so much money."

"And I got them to give you more."

"Yeah. That's why I pay you the big bucks." Charlie brought Brady a beer and Leo a Manhattan. They clinked glasses. "To seven figures and five books," Max said.

"I'm still in shock I agreed to that many."

"Why did you?"

He shrugged his shoulders, trying to rid himself of the weight he felt due to the choices he'd made. "I told you. I'm done with cookbooks. I'll have a lot of time on my hands." And this way, he wouldn't be tempted to let Clare give up her dream. In any case, he was excited about this new series of books. It was geared to older kids and had some magic in it. Brady needed a clean slate everywhere.

"Cheer up, boy. When you're the next J. K. Rowling, you'll be a bigger star than she ever thought of being with the cooking thing."

"Yeah, sure," he said, slugging back his beer. "That'd make me feel great."

AT THE END OF THE WEEK, Jonathan awoke from a fitful sleep, depressed and guilty. This wasn't working. He climbed out of bed and made his way to the bathroom. In the mirror over the sink, he could barely look himself in the eye. It had been four days since Langston had come to the office, four days since the man had confronted Jonathan, wanting the truth.

And Jonathan had lied. He'd tried to confess, but he couldn't, and the demons he'd kept at bay for weeks refused to be quelled any longer. Because of that, in the cold light of day, he could no longer hold his head up.

Trying to push away the thoughts, he finished in the bathroom and found his way to the kitchen. Coffee helped wake him up, but it also made him jittery. He kept seeing Clarissa, sick in the Marriott bathroom, shaking in the hotel room, fearful and anxious on the flight back. And he had the power, the knowledge, to make it all better. He turned and stared out at the backyard of his house. As he watched the birds at the birdfeeder, he admitted some things to himself: the most important was the fact that he could no longer keep the last piece of the puzzle from her. He did love Clarissa as much as Langston did, and it was time to start acting that way.

CLARE WAS LYING ON THE COUCH in her living room watching no-mind TV when the doorbell rang. She'd gotten home early this morning, after a surprisingly restful night.

She and Lillian had had breakfast outside under the umbrella table. The chirping of the birds and the warmth of the morning had soothed Clare's frayed nerves. They'd talked a lot about Brady's dad, and Brady himself, but it hadn't upset Clare.

The bell rang again just as she reached the door. The peephole revealed it was Jonathan. A bolt of fear went though Clare, confusing her. The calm she'd experienced with Lillian this morning evaporated, and she was reluctant to let him in. But she owed Jonathan that much. Besides, she needed to tell him the decision she'd finally been able to make.

He looked terrible. She'd never seen him with a growth of beard, other than when she'd woken up in the morning with him. And his shirt and pants were wrinkled. "Jonathan, hi. Are you all right?"

"No. Can I come in?"

She held open the door. "Of course."

In the foyer, he paced and ran an agitated hand over his face.

"Come in and sit down."

"I want to stand."

"Okay. Let's go into the living room." He followed her inside, and she leaned against the back of the chair. "What has you so upset?"

"I'm not the man Brady Langston is, Clarissa."

"Jonathan, if this is about—"

"Let me finish! This is hard enough as it is."

She wrapped her arms around her waist, remembering the alligator, sensing danger.

"Langston came to see me before he left," Jonathan told her abruptly.

"Why?"

"For information. About what happened right before the accident."

Clare thought of the theory Anna, Cathy and Brady had, that Jonathan had insisted on sex, and Clare's conscious mind couldn't deal with the aftermath. Could he possibly be here to confirm that? She pressed her hand over her mouth.

"I didn't exactly lie to you that night in New York. I simply left some things out. It was all true, but something else happened before you left."

"Wh-what?"

"You told me you were sorry for what you did. And I..." He drew in a heavy breath.

No, please, this couldn't be what the others thought. "You what?"

"I did tell you I could forgive you. I did ask you to marry me, but you insisted things weren't all right. You said you'd done something unconscionable, but..."

"But?"

His throat convulsed as if he couldn't get the words out. "But that you'd driven around a while after you left Langston and realized something. That you didn't regret what you'd done with him because it made you realize how you really felt."

"That I loved you, right?"

His eyes closed briefly. "No, damn it, that you loved *him*. You told me you wanted to be with him, and if he'd have you, you were going back to him." The words were wrenched from Jonathan, his tone a combination of real sorrow tinged with an underlying bitterness.

It was like getting hit by a lightning bolt. The scene came to her in living color...

SHE WAS STANDING in the living room of his big colonial across the city. "I'm sorry that I cheated on you, Jonathan. But I love Brady."

Jonathan looked shocked. "No, I won't accept this. How can you even think about leaving me?"

"I'm sorry, but you'll have to accept it."

"What kind of person are you, that you would do this?

He'd hit her Achilles' heel. She started to cry.

"Don't you *dare* cry over another man in front of me."

"Please, I—"

"Get out of here. I can't stand to watch you suffer over him."

She was crying so hard she could barely see straight. "I need to call Brady. I'm too upset to drive."

"You have to call *him?* You'd tell me this now?" Enraged, he flung the liquor glass he'd been sipping from across the room, smashing it against the fireplace. "For God's sake, Clarissa, just get out of here."

CLARE STARED AT HIM. It wasn't as bad as it could have been, and he didn't deserve the awful suspicions everybody had had about him. But he should have told her all of it. What he'd done when she'd gotten amnesia was inexcusable. He knew she'd chosen Brady and he'd tried to win her back. And under the circumstances, pushing her to make love with him was totally wrong.

"I caused your accident, Clarissa."

With startling clarity, Clare realized that in some ways he had. "You should have told me this before." Her voice was heated.

"You're right to be angry. You chose him, and I sent you out into the night upset. I'm a horrible person."

For the first time, she could see his crippling guilt. Though it would take her a long time to forgive him, she wouldn't add to it. And she bore some guilt for what she'd done. What good would all these recriminations do, anyway?

"I know you were upset by what I'd done, Jonathan. Rightfully so. And you didn't know I'd left my cell phone at home. That I'd drive, after all."

"Until right now, I didn't know that's *why* you drove."

"It doesn't matter anymore. There's blame on both sides. I acted badly, too, when I made love with Brady."

He shook his head, his eyes bleak, his whole posture sagging. "I guess it doesn't." He stared at her a long time. "This is the end of us, then."

"It is."

After a long hesitation, he said simply, "Goodbye, Clarissa."

"Goodbye, Jonathan."

As she watched him leave, Clare knew the decision she'd made earlier was the right one. Finally, she knew what she would do.

CLARE HAD HAD A HELL OF A TIME finding Brady. She called his sister Sam, who scoffed at her, hounded Delia and Max, though they were cold and not forthcoming, and even checked with Lucinda, who laughed into the phone, then hung up.

She was just about to call Lillian when help came unexpectedly. Donny Kramer arrived at her condo without Delia.

Despite the situation, she was glad to see someone who still loved her. "Donny, what are you doing here?"

"I know where Uncle Brady is," he blurted out. "I heard you asking Mom, and she wouldn't tell you."

"Oh, honey, I don't want you in the middle of this. I'll find him another way."

Donny went on despite her objection. "He saw me before he left. He said he was going away. He's in New York, the place you always stayed at."

Swallowing hard at the boy's loyalty to her, Clare had hugged Donny until he was embarrassed.

Without packing, she drove to the airport and got the first flight to New York that was available. When she landed, she made a stop on Madison Avenue, then she headed to Charlie's Pub.

The old man grinned hugely when he saw her come through the door. He'd aged since the last time she'd been here two years ago. "There she is," he said warmly, as if she'd been coming to the pub routinely. "I asked Brady how you were, but he didn't tell me much." He frowned. "I've missed you, girl. You all right?"

"I missed you, too." She gave him an impulsive peck on the cheek. "And I'm fine. I'm wonderful. He's here, right?"

"Yeah, upstairs. Been moping around like a puppy for days. You got anything to do with that?"

"Yep."

"You gonna fix it?"

"Uh-huh."

He pulled out a drawer and handed her a key. "Go for it. The second suite."

Clare sprinted up the back stairs to the floor where Brady was staying. Her heart pounded as she neared the door, and not from the exercise. Should she knock? No. Better to surprise him.

She heard the shower running when she walked into the living area. Not much had changed since she'd last stayed here. The space was uncluttered, with a slightly worn couch, a stuffed recliner, a braided rug on the floor and a

TV. Mementos of Charlie's life hung on the walls, giving the place a homey feeling. She sniffed. It smelled familiar. Wonderfully familiar.

The bath was off the bedroom, so she headed in there. Again, the room was furnished in a homey decor, a lot like Brady's room, where she'd slept last night. She dropped down on the big oak bed, brimming with anticipation.

Five minutes later Brady came into the room, staring down at the floor, with a towel wrapped around his waist, his hair wet and his body gleaming. A rush of desire hit Clare so hard she gasped, making him look up.

His face went from surprise to displeasure to resignation. "What are you doing here, Clare?"

"I've come to bring you back home."

"New York's my new home."

"Like hell."

"I signed a huge book deal."

"Good for you." She crossed her ankles at her feet and smiled. "You'll have to set your deadlines around our cookbooks."

He shook his head. "I'm done with them."

"No, you aren't."

FROM THE OTHER SIDE of the room, Brady watched Clare, nonplussed at why she'd come. She wouldn't hurt him like this intentionally just to get her way. "Wait a sec. I can't have this conversation half-naked." He went to the closet, turned his back to her, pulled out jeans, dropped the towel and dragged them on commando.

What the hell? She whistled at the sight of his bare butt? That made him mad.

He whirled around. "What's wrong with you? Don't you

know I can barely put one foot in front of the other these days? Why are you here, acting like this?"

She shrugged a shoulder, not in the least chagrined by his tirade. "I'm going to help you walk again, I guess."

He was so tired of all this that the fight went out of him. "Just tell me why you're here, Clare. Don't play games, and don't be so damn happy."

"I can't help being happy." She stood and approached him. For the life of him, he couldn't decipher the look in her eyes. She was dressed in plain jeans and a nice blazer. She looked casual and cute and so good it made his heart ache even more. Damn her.

"I went to see the Cooking Channel people before I came to Charlie's."

Ah, so that was it. God, how could she be so obtuse? Didn't she know this was killing him?

"It doesn't matter if they relinquished their demands about the cookbooks. I can't work with you again." His voice rose on the last, but how much could a man take? "I already told you this, damn it."

"They didn't relinquish their demands. It was a deal breaker." She held up her palms. "So I broke the deal."

"I told you I wouldn't let you do that. This is what you always wanted."

"You didn't *let* me do anything. This is totally my decision. I've done it. And it isn't the end of my dream, Brade. There are other TV stations, other syndications. The Cooking Channel isn't the only game in town."

"They're the best."

"Then I'll settle for second best. About that." She moved in to him and slid her hands up his bare chest, making every nerve in his body tingle. "Because I'll have you. And you, Brady Langston, are clearly numero uno."

He swallowed hard. "What happened to bring all this on?"

"I remember everything from the night of the accident. You were right. Jonathan was lying. Well, keeping something from me."

His fists curled at his sides. "I'll kill the bastard."

"He's not a bastard. He's hurt and a lot worse off than we are now."

Grabbing her hands, Brady was afraid of what she'd tell him, but he had to know. "I need the details, Clare. Now. And whatever it is, I'll help you deal with it."

When she finished describing the events of that night, he shook his head. "So the cause of your amnesia was physical?"

"Maybe not. Maybe I *was* so torn by what we did, I couldn't remember the scene with Jonathan. Anyway, what does it matter? The amnesia's gone."

"Oh, man. I wouldn't want to be in Harris's shoes. I'd never forgive myself."

"You know what? I think everybody needs to forgive everything that's been done here."

Brady almost didn't know what to do with the relief that flooded him.

Almost.

"You do, huh?" He placed his hands on her hips and yanked her close. He was aroused, mightily, and he wanted her to know it. "Here's what I think. I think you should kiss me." He put his lips to her forehead. "Then I think you should take off all those clothes, so this time I can get a good look at you, naked and beautiful." His hands were already on the snap of her jeans. He leaned in and steeped himself in the feel and scent of her. "And we should make love—slow, intimate, earth-shattering love."

"You know, Brady, I remember how I always liked that about you. You're a man who's not afraid to say what he thinks." She whispered, "A man who's not afraid to take what he wants."

He sobered and peered into her incredible eyes. "I want you, Clare. Now and always." His throat clogged. "I love you so much."

"I love you, too." Her voice shook with emotion. "I'm sorry it took so long for me to realize it."

He kissed her nose. "There was that little matter of amnesia."

"A twist of fate, Brady, that in the end brought us together."

He buried his face in her neck. "We'll have to toast to fate. Later."

"Hmm," Clare said, holding on to him tightly. "Much, much later."

* * * * *

*Celebrate 60 years of pure reading pleasure
with Harlequin Books!*

*Harlequin Romance is celebrating by s
howering you with* DIAMOND BRIDES
*in February 2009.
Six stories that promise to bring a
touch of sparkle to your life, with
diamond proposals and dazzling weddings,
sparkling brides and gorgeous grooms!*

Enjoy a sneak peek at Caroline Anderson's
TWO LITTLE MIRACLES,
*available February 2009
from Harlequin Romance.*

'I'VE FOUND HER.'

Max froze.

It was what he'd been waiting for since June, but now—now he was almost afraid to voice the question. His heart stalling, he leaned slowly back in his chair and scoured the investigator's face for clues. 'Where?' he asked, and his voice sounded rough and unused, like a rusty hinge.

'In Suffolk. She's living in a cottage.'

Living. His heart crashed back to life, and he sucked in a long, slow breath. All these months he'd feared—

'Is she well?'

'Yes, she's well.'

He had to force himself to ask the next question. 'Alone?'

The man paused. 'No. The cottage belongs to a man called John Blake. He's working away at the moment, but he comes and goes.'

God. He felt sick. So sick he hardly registered the next few words, but then gradually they sank in. 'She's got *what?*'

'Babies. Twin girls. They're eight months old.'

'Eight—?' he echoed under his breath. 'They must be his.'

He was thinking out loud, but the P.I. heard and corrected him.

'Apparently not. I gather they're hers. She's been there since mid-January last year, and they were born during the summer—June, the woman in the post office thought. She was more than helpful. I think there's been a certain amount of speculation about their relationship.'

He'd just bet there had. God, he was going to kill her. Or Blake. Maybe both of them.

'Of course, looking at the dates, she was presumably pregnant when she left you, so they could be yours, or she could have been having an affair with this Blake character before…'

He glared at the unfortunate P.I. 'Just stick to your job. I can do the math,' he snapped, swallowing the unpalatable possibility that she'd been unfaithful to him before she'd left. 'Where is she? I want the address.'

'It's all in here,' the man said, sliding a large envelope across the desk to him. 'With my invoice.'

'I'll get it seen to. Thank you.'

'If there's anything else you need, Mr Gallagher, any further information—'

'I'll be in touch.'

'The woman in the post office told me Blake was away at the moment, if that helps,' he added quietly, and opened the door.

Max stared down at the envelope, hardly daring to open it, but when the door clicked softly shut behind the P.I., he eased up the flap, tipped it and felt his breath jam in his throat as the photos spilled out over the desk.

Oh, lord, she looked gorgeous. Different, though. It took him a moment to recognise her, because she'd grown her hair, and it was tied back in a ponytail, making her look younger and somehow freer. The blond highlights were gone, and it was back to its natural soft golden-brown, with a little curl in the end of the ponytail that he wanted to thread his finger through and tug, just gently, to draw her back to him.

Crazy. She'd put on a little weight, but it suited her. She looked well and happy and beautiful, but oddly, considering how desperate he'd been for news of her for the past year—one year, three weeks and two days, to be exact—it wasn't only Julia who held his attention after the initial shock. It was the babies sitting side by side in a supermarket trolley. Two identical and absolutely beautiful little girls.

* * * * *

When Max Gallagher hires a P.I. to find his estranged wife, Julia, he discovers she's not alone—she has twin baby girls, and they might be his. Now workaholic Max has just two weeks to prove that he can be a wonderful husband and father to the family he wants to treasure.

Look for TWO LITTLE MIRACLES
by Caroline Anderson,
available February 2009
from Harlequin Romance.

CELEBRATE
60 YEARS
OF PURE READING PLEASURE
WITH HARLEQUIN®!

We'll be spotlighting a different series
every month throughout 2009
to celebrate our 60th anniversary.

Look for Harlequin® Romance in February!

**Harlequin® Romance is celebrating by showering
you with Diamond Brides in February 2009.**

Six stories that promise to bring a touch of sparkle to
your life, with diamond proposals and dazzling weddings,
sparkling brides and gorgeous grooms!

Collect all six books in February 2009,
featuring *Two Little Miracles* by Caroline Anderson.

*Look for the Diamond Brides miniseries
in February 2009!*

HARLEQUIN® *Romance*®

This February the Harlequin® Romance series
will feature six Diamond Brides stories featuring
diamond proposals and gorgeous grooms.

Share your dream wedding proposal and you could WIN!

The most romantic entry will win a diamond
necklace and will inspire a proposal in one of
our upcoming Diamond Grooms books in 2010.

In 100 words or less, tell us the most romantic
way that you dream of being proposed to.

For more information, and to enter
the Diamond Brides Proposal contest, please visit
www.DiamondBridesProposal.com

Or mail your entry to us at:

IN THE U.S.: 3010 Walden Ave., P.O. Box 9069, Buffalo, NY 14269-9069
IN CANADA: 225 Duncan Mill Road, Don Mills, ON M3B 3K9

REQUEST YOUR FREE BOOKS!
2 FREE NOVELS PLUS 2 FREE GIFTS!

HARLEQUIN®

Super Romance®

Exciting, emotional, unexpected!

YES! Please send me 2 FREE Harlequin Superromance® novels and my 2 FREE gifts (gifts are worth about $10). After receiving them, if I don't wish to receive any more books, I can return the shipping statement marked "cancel." If I don't cancel, I will receive 6 brand-new novels every month and be billed just $4.69 per book in the U.S. or $5.24 per book in Canada, plus 25¢ shipping and handling per book and applicable taxes, if any*. That's a savings of close to 15% off the cover price! I understand that accepting the 2 free books and gifts places me under no obligation to buy anything. I can always return a shipment and cancel at any time. Even if I never buy another book from Harlequin, the two free books and gifts are mine to keep forever.

135 HDN EEX7 336 HDN EEYK

Name	(PLEASE PRINT)	
Address		Apt. #
City	State/Prov.	Zip/Postal Code

Signature (if under 18, a parent or guardian must sign)

Mail to the Harlequin Reader Service:
IN U.S.A.: P.O. Box 1867, Buffalo, NY 14240-1867
IN CANADA: P.O. Box 609, Fort Erie, Ontario L2A 5X3

Not valid to current subscribers of Harlequin Superromance books.

Want to try two free books from another line?
Call 1-800-873-8635 or visit www.morefreebooks.com.

* Terms and prices subject to change without notice. N.Y. residents add applicable sales tax. Canadian residents will be charged applicable provincial taxes and GST. Offer not valid in Quebec. This offer is limited to one order per household. All orders subject to approval. Credit or debit balances in a customer's account(s) may be offset by any other outstanding balance owed by or to the customer. Please allow 4 to 6 weeks for delivery. Offer available while quantities last.

Your Privacy: Harlequin is committed to protecting your privacy. Our Privacy Policy is available online at www.eHarlequin.com or upon request from the Reader Service. From time to time we make our lists of customers available to reputable third parties who may have a product or service of interest to you. If you would prefer we not share your name and address, please check here. ☐

HSR08R

You're invited to join our Tell Harlequin Reader Panel!

By joining our new reader panel you will:

- Receive Harlequin® books—they are FREE and yours to keep with no obligation to purchase anything!
- Participate in fun online surveys
- Exchange opinions and ideas with women just like you
- Have a say in our new book ideas and help us publish the best in women's fiction

In addition, you will have a chance to win great prizes and receive special gifts!
See Web site for details. Some conditions apply.
Space is limited.

To join, visit us at
www.TellHarlequin.com.

HARLEQUIN

Super Romance

COMING NEXT MONTH

#1542 THE STORY BETWEEN THEM • Molly O'Keefe
Jennifer Stern has left journalism to focus on life with her son. Then
Ian Greer—son of a former president—picks her to tell the true story of
his family, and it's a scoop she can't resist. But could her attraction to Ian
jeopardize the piece?

#1543 A COWBOY'S REDEMPTION • Jeannie Watt
Home on the Ranch
Kira Jennings just wants access across Jason Ross's land so she can subdivide
her property and sell it off…and save face with her CEO, aka grandfather.
Sure, there's bad blood between Jason and her brother. She didn't realize
exactly *how* bad. Until now.

#1544 THE HERO'S SIN • Darlene Gardner
Return to Indigo Springs
Good thing Sarah Brenneman doesn't judge a book by its cover. Otherwise she'd
believe what the town's gossips say about Michael Donahue. Instead, she's
impressed by his heroics. Still, can she believe what her heart is telling her
about Michael, or could those rumors end their romance before it even begins?

#1545 A KID TO THE RESCUE • Susan Gable
Suddenly a Parent
Shannon Vanderhoff knows that everybody and everything are temporary
gifts. So when she becomes guardian of her six-year-old, traumatized nephew,
how can she give him the help he needs without falling for him? It takes
Greg Hawkins's art therapy class to turn the child around…and it takes a kid
to create this loving family.

#1546 THE THINGS WE DO FOR LOVE • Margot Early
The man Mary Anne Drew loves is marrying someone else. So she buys a love
potion to win him back. Too bad the wrong man drinks it! Graham Corbett has
never shown any interest in Mary Anne before. Could the potion really work?
Or was she looking for love in the wrong place all along?

#1547 WHAT FAMILY MEANS • Geri Krotow
Everlasting Love
Debra and Will Bradley wanted their kids to know that family means
everything. Through hard and joyous times, Debra and Will have never
questioned that. Now Angie, their daughter, is pregnant—and separated.
Award-winning author Geri Krotow tells a memorable story of how marriage
and family define our lives.